GENTLEMAN'S PROPOSITION . . .

Linda had been wandering about in the rain, her feet cold in her thin shoes, wondering where she could go without a cent in her pocket.

Then, suddenly, she was being driven in Sir Sydney's Rolls, sipping brandy in his large library, warming her cold feet by the fire—with him looking on concernedly.

"I've got a suggestion," he said. "I will offer it to you as an alternative to walking about in the rain." For a moment the fierce but handsome Sir Sydney looked embarrassed. "What about coming to live with me here?" he finally said.

LOVE AND LINDA

Barbara Cartland

PYRAMID BOOKS ▲ **NEW YORK**

LOVE AND LINDA

A PYRAMID BOOK

Copyright © 1976 by Barbara Cartland

Pyramid edition published July 1976

Printed in the United States of America

Pyramid Books are published by Pyramid Publications (Harcourt
Brace Jovanovich). Its trademarks, consisting of the word
"Pyramid" and the portrayal of a pyramid, are registered in the
United States Patent Office.

Pyramid Publications
(Harcourt Brace Jovanovich)
757 Third Avenue, New York, N.Y. 10017

LOVE AND LINDA

REFLECTION ONE

1928

Mummy's first words to me:

"Here's a pretty kettle of fish, Linda!"

And she's right. But there is no need for her to worry, she's in clover, I've got to do the worrying—about myself.

Not that Mummy is not fussed, I think she is.

But what with all the excitement about her wedding and her anxiety that Bill Blomfield shan't be troubled by me, one can't expect her to be awfully upset about the future of a daughter she has only seen two or three times in the last six years.

Mummy has altered a lot since the days I used to think her beautiful, when I stood shivering in the wings while she was performing.

How cold it used to be sometimes! But it was the excitement I liked.

I suppose any child would have liked it—the anxiety and thrill of the opening performance and the fun and jolliness of everyone on a Saturday night, even though a lot of them were a bit tipsy.

The Stage Manager always was; I can't remember a Saturday at any of the places where we went to when the Stage Manager was not what Alfred used to call "half-seas over".

Alfred had often had a couple himself, too, and one evening he forgot to see that the trapeze was properly set up by the stage hands, it toppled over and he hurt his knee.

We had to cancel the whole of our next month's engagements because he couldn't hang from the bar and swing Mummy by her feet with his knee stiff and bandaged.

Alfred was a nice man, even though he did knock Mummy about sometimes when he was jealous of her.

How I used to hate those rows! They used to haunt me for years after I had been at the Convent. I would wake up shivering with fright.

Yet I liked Alfred. He fascinated me with his long waxed moustache, the muscles bulging on his arms when he squared his shoulders, and his conquering air as he marched up and down before the audience in red satin trunks covered with gold stars.

He was kind, too, in his own way, and often gave me a penny to buy sweets when he was in a good humour. All the years I knew him he never hit me, which is more than I could say of Mummy.

I wonder what would have happened to me if I had gone on living with them? I suppose I would have gone into the trapeze business, too, in the end, though Mummy was dead against it.

Alfred used to try and make me exercise to get my limbs supple, but if Mummy caught him at it there were always words:

"Linda isn't going into anything without a future in it," she used to say; "her father was a gentleman, and I'm not going to have her mucking about on the boards all her life!"

Then Alfred used to strike an attitude and curl his moustache.

"Quite a little Vere de Vere! What's good enough for

her mother ain't good enough for her ladyship, I suppose! It's a pity her father, being the nob he was, didn't leave her something in his will—even if it was only his name!"

At that Mummy would lose her temper and scream at him, and it always ended more or less in the same way with her saying:

"Bastard or no bastard I will thank you to keep your hands off my child and mind your own business!"

As I got older I often asked Mummy about this "gentleman" father of mine, but she has always been secretive about him.

It happened when she was quite young and had a good part in the chorus of one of the big London theatres.

But after I had spoilt her career, so to speak, she couldn't get in again with the right agents and was glad to take up with some acrobats doing a tour of the Halls.

She has always been double-jointed—her mother was before her—and it did not take her long to pick up enough tricks to give quite a creditable performance, though Alfred told me she would never be first-class, not having started when she was a child.

It was some years later that Alfred and his "Scarlet Swallows" happened along, and he fell for Mummy—as a woman of course, not as an artist—and she joined him and became a Swallow too.

Alfred was doing well in those days touring the first-class Halls, but I can only remember when they had come down a bit and were content to play in very third-rate places.

I have always had a suspicion that this was due to Mummy; she was terribly jealous of Alfred and gradually ousted all the younger girls from the turn.

She insisted on doing most of Alfred's tricks with him, and as she was never a top-notcher, the show was bound to suffer.

Dimly in the past I remember a pretty dark-haired little "Swallow" packing her trunk and having a few parting words with Mummy before she left the troupe.

Alfred took no part in the repartee, which got louder and louder between the two women.

He never did take sides unless the combatants came to blows, and on this occasion he stood back twirling his long moustache and looking the very picture of strong manhood.

There had been many rows like this before and he was used to them. The young Swallow made her exit with a last shot at Mummy:

"Call yourself a swallow?" she said, "more like a flying rhinoceros with those hips!"

With that she flounced out of the theatre while Mummy screamed some incoherent reply about her ancestry and her looks.

I enjoyed those days, there were always new people to make a fuss of me, to give me sweets or to pay me a penny for the messages I could run for them between the acts.

It was a funny life for a child. Mummy and Alfred used to sleep till eleven or twelve o'clock in the morning unless there was a rehearsal, and although I was awake I used to have to lie quiet as a mouse for fear of waking them.

I hardly dared move or turn over, for the wicker property basket would creak like anything if I did.

So I used to tell myself stories until with grunts and groans one of them would stretch and yawn noisily, and I would know that a new day had begun.

Most of the day they slopped about in the bedroom, sending down for a large steak and a couple of bottles of stout if we were in funds. The steak I would help them with, but I hated stout, in spite of Alfred's coaxing.

"Come on, Linda," he would say. "Drink it up, it'll give you some roses in your cheeks—you look half-starved. I can't say as how you're an advertisement for the prosperity of the 'Scarlet Swallows'."

Nice, kind Alfred! I wonder where he is now? A year ago Mummy said he had gone to America, but whether that was true or just to save her face, I wasn't certain.

I wasn't with them when the split came. It was all on account of Mummy breaking her leg. She was getting stiff and she never could stand swinging head downwards for long, it always made her giddy, and one day she fell.

Of course Alfred had to get someone else for the troupe, and it wasn't likely, in spite of anything Mummy could say, that he was going to get anyone old.

Apparently Mummy didn't trust her from the first, and rightly, for in a month she had Alfred completely under

10

her thumb and Mummy was a back number.

The poor dear didn't have a chance lying there with her broken leg, and as they couldn't afford to cart her about with them, or stop the tour, she had to be left behind.

When she was better she came North to visit me at the convent. One of the few occasions she came to see me all the time I was there.

It semed odd to watch Mummy, who had always been so active, hobbling along on a couple of sticks. Her leg was mending, but it was still stiff and she couldn't walk without them.

She was all dressed up, but she couldn't disguise her face, and almost as soon as she arrived I knew something had happened.

"What's the matter, Mummy?" I asked.

She told me then that Alfred had gone off with some "fancy" woman, and the next time she wrote she said he had gone to America "and a good riddance, too!"

But I shouldn't be surprised if Alfred just told her that to keep her from following him: Mummy was quite capable of turning up and making a scene.

I am glad I wasn't there when Mummy broke her leg. I used to feel physically sick in case she did fall, especially when she waved and giggled at the audience instead of counting as Alfred had told her to.

But before all this had happened my life had changed considerably.

There had been an awful fuss after the War about the education of children, and in every town we visited we were continually being rounded up by Inspectors to enquire about my education.

I used to keep out of their way as much as possible, but sometimes I had to go to school for two or three days until we moved on again.

I could hardly read, but I could add up pennies quick enough and could sing any amount of comic songs. I had a whole repertoire of them that I had learnt from listening night after night at the Halls.

Well, we had settled in one of the north-country towns for a fortnight and I had avoided school for three days. It was Friday evening and we were all on the stage dismantling the trapeze, the "Scarlet Swallows" being the last

11

turn on the bill, when in comes the Inspector and starts kicking up a row.

He tells Mummy it is disgraceful how little I know and that he is going to get an injunction so that I would be compelled to stay in one place and be taught properly.

Thereupon Mummy turned on him like a wild cat:

"You can't take a child from its mother. Is that the law or isn't it, I should like to know?"

The Inspector began to get annoyed and the troupe all came round, saying what they thought, and I started to cry, which I had always found effective when my schooling was in question.

The Inspector got more and more annoyed, and then Alfred offered to fight him.

Alfred was still in his scarlet trunks, but he had put on a short coat when he had finished his act and he started to take it off, while the two girls and Mummy egged him on.

One of the men said:

"Don't be a B.F., Alfred, you'll get into trouble; he's got the law on his side."

And just at that moment along comes the Manager of the theatre accompanied by a lady, and naturally they stopped and asked what all the hullabaloo was about.

Everyone in the company tried to explain, and I began to enjoy all this excitement over me. With my arms round Mummy's waist I sobbed:

"I don't want to leave my mother and go to school, I don't want to leave my mother!"

The lady with the Manager was quite old, about fifty or sixty I should say. She was well dressed in a quiet way with a dark sable fur and magnificent pearls round her neck.

I was to learn later her name was Mrs. Fisher-Simmonds, that she was very well known for her charitable works and was always arranging matinées for this or that cause, inveigling managers to lend their theatres and artistes to give their services.

Having grasped the meaning of what was going on, she held out her hand to me and said:

"Come here, little girl."

I went towards her wide-eyed and rather curious as to what was going to happen.

I was over eleven at the time but I looked younger, and

I suppose I was a very pretty child with masses of fair curly hair, wide grey eyes, and a small tip-tilted nose which has never got much bigger.

I was not only small for my age, I was also very thin and pale for lack of proper food and fresh air.

Mrs. Fisher-Simmonds touched my cheek and said:

"This child looks to me under-nourished," which annoyed Mummy and she retorted:

"Linda has the best we can afford; if you expect her to have oysters and champagne every day you'd better speak to the Manager!"

The lady took no notice of Mummy's rudeness, but talked to me for a few minutes, asking questions which seemed to me to have little bearing on the matter at hand.

I was very much on my guard, terrified of showing my ignorance, and not particularly affable.

I was astonished as we walked back towards the group, standing almost in silence by this time as if awaiting a verdict, to hear Mrs. Fisher-Simmonds announce:

"I have decided that I will see to this child's education; she shall go to a Convent in which I am interested where she will be properly looked after. Bring her to my house tomorrow afternoon at three o'clock and I will make all arrangements."

For a moment everyone was too astounded to speak, and then the Inspector murmured that in that case, everything was settled as far as he was concerned, while I burst into genuine tears.

I had no desire to be properly taught, least of all in a Convent; I didn't know what it was, but it sounded like another sort of prison.

Visions of myself in long black garments rushed to my mind.

I started to protest, only to be seized by Mummy and shaken into silence.

"Thank you, M'am," she said to Mrs. Fisher-Simmonds, "I will bring Linda to-morrow as you say."

She took the card the lady held out and then the Manager and Mrs. Fisher-Simmonds disappeared from the stage.

There was a moment's silence punctuated only by my sobs, and then everyone started talking at once:

"What an opportunity!" "What luck!" "Wasn't I fortunate!"

But I wouldn't listen; stuffing my fingers in my ears I screamed at them:

"I don't want to go to a Convent."

But I was only given a sharp slap from Mummy, followed by another until I subsided on the stage at her feet.

"You little fool," she said, "you don't know what is good for you, most girls would give they eyes for a chance like this!"

"And now," she said, turning to Alfred in triumph, "perhaps you will believe Linda has good blood in her."

She dragged me off to the lodgings, talking nineteen to the dozen:

"The Lord knows what you will wear, you have grown out of your red *crêpe de Chine*—perhaps I've got time to cut down my green velvet for you, with a lace collar—that'd be sweet. You don't want to be too flashy, just ladylike; after all, if you are going to live among the ladies you want to look like one of them."

But I could take no interest in my appearance and that night I sobbed myself to sleep, curled up in the old prop basket for the last time.

The property basket had for a long time been too small for me, and when we were lucky enough to have a room that had a couch in it, I slept on that.

But such luxuries were few and far between, for our digs got cheaper and cheaper as time went on, and even the bottles of stout had been cut down as engagements got fewer and less well paid.

It was by a lucky chance as it happens, though I did not realise it at the time, that the "Scarlet Swallows" had been booked for that particular week at the theatre where we met Mrs. Fisher-Simmonds.

Some well-known acrobats who were to have figured on the bill had cancelled the engagement at the last moment.

The Manager had wired to his London agents to send another turn of the same kind.

That was how the "Scarlet Swallows" had fallen in on a job that was right out of their class, a job which, as it happens, was to alter the entire course of my life.

Mrs. Fisher-Simmonds had a house in the best residential part of the town, and she was one of the life governors of the Roman Catholic Convent which was built some two miles out in the country.

The Convent of the Sacred Hands had been endowed for the daughters of poor clergymen, doctors and solicitors. But each governor could nominate one free pupil every five years.

Mrs. Fisher-Simmonds was a big noise in the neighborhood, and any decision of hers was unlikely to be queried or frustrated.

Otherwise there would surely have been an outcry at my entering the convent, for the day girls were all daughters of well-to-do trades-people and local professional men, while the boarders were one and all of a far better social position than me.

In the years to come I was to realise, however, that Mrs. Fisher-Simmonds rather enjoyed showing her powers by doing small things which would arouse antagonism and argument from everyone else.

She liked to see people gulp back their protests because it was her decision, whatever it might be. While as far as the Convent was concerned I was to learn that she was considered a holy terror and that everyone in the place was afraid of her.

I shall never forget the awful terrifying loneliness when I was first left in the grey stone building which seemed to me a prison from which I should never be able to escape.

I clung to Mummy in floods of tears and she was crying herself as she walked away down the drive, turning back to wave to me as I stood holding a tear-sodden handkerchief in one hand, the other clasped firmly by a Nun.

After I had settled down, which was not for some months, I really quite enjoyed the life.

I began to grow as the good food and exercise altered my constitution, but I suffered at first through being so backward.

I had to start in the baby class amongst children six and seven, for I was hopelessly ignorant, except where taking care of myself was concerned. At that I was adept and I soon stopped any form of teasing.

Of course I was punished for scratching, kicking and for using language which horrified the Nuns, but in some curious way the girls respected me for my savageness.

Of course, I was hideously homesick and Mummy's

15

letters (which were few and far between, badly spelt and often unintelligible) made things worse; they never told me the things I wanted to know.

Then she and Alfred came to visit me when they were in a nearby town, and it seemed to me that the old relationship had been completely broken between us.

I had been so excited at their coming, almost hysterical when I heard there was even a possibility of seeing them, that the actual meeting was an anticlimax.

They came dressed in their best, slightly awkward, and nervous not only of the Nuns and the peeping girls at every window, but also of me.

My cleanness, neatness and altered appearance upset them, they missed the ragged noisy uncouth Linda who had slept at the bottom of their bed night after night.

Alfred never came again, and that was the last time I saw him, and I hate to think of him, sitting on the edge of a chair, in an ill-fitting suit, twiddling his bowler hat.

I like to remember him in red and spangles, with waxed moustache, and his sleek hair oiled into a quiff, his muscles bulging as he raised himself on the trapeze.

Mrs. Fisher-Simmonds was delighted with me as the years passed. She used to come over once a month to patronise the whole place, and always asked especially for me.

"Perhaps she will leave you something in her will," one of the girls suggested.

From that moment I used to tell myself stories in which I was left thousands of pounds by my kind benefactor and went back to the troupe rich and important.

I dreamt of the parties I would give with unlimited bottles of stout and outsize steaks!

The girls at the Convent were all trained for different professions, many of them were to be governesses, some were to go on to schools of music or needlework, while others wished to be lady-gardeners or secretaries.

As I was not proficient at any of these things there seemed some difficulty as to my future, but when I asked the Mother Superior she said:

"I think Mrs. Fisher-Simmonds has definite plans for you, Linda".

When I first went to the Convent they tried to call me by my proper name, which is, of course, Belinda, but I fought for the name I had always known of "Linda."

Although the Nuns held out for some time, they were forced after a while to submit to the inevitable as all the girls called me Linda, and I made a pretence of not hearing if addressed as "Belinda".

Mrs. Fisher-Simmonds said nothing to me about the future, and I was far too frightened of her, as everyone else was, to ask her point-blank.

Then a fortnight ago they told us that she was seriously ill and special prayers and Masses were said for her in the Chapel.

I have already outstayed my allotted time at the school, for most of the girls leave when they are seventeen, while I shall be eighteen next month.

I haven't heard from Mummy for four or five months. She wrote that she had got a job as a barmaid at the "Cross Keys" in North London, but since then, silence.

However, the "Cross Keys" found her when the news finally came that Mrs. Fisher-Simmonds was dead and had left me—nothing.

There was no mention of me at all in her will, nor in the instructions she left for her son who has inherited everything she possessed.

Ten days after she was buried the Mother Superior sent for me and told me that I must now make some choice as to what I would do.

They would do their best to get me a position as they always did with their girls. But, she added, it was a pity I had not specialised in any particular branch of their education, and she blamed herself for being led away by ideas and fancies as to what Mrs. Fisher-Simmonds intended.

I made up my mind there and then to get out of the Convent and fend for myself.

I wrote to Mummy that very afternoon, saying that she must ask for me and insist on my coming home to her, wherever she was. If my letter was a surprise, her reply gave me a bit of a shock:

> *"Linda, dearie, I am sorry to hear the old lady
> is dead and has left you nothing. Come here to
> see me if you want to, but I can't promise any-
> thing as I am going to marry Bill Blomfield who*

owns this pub and we won't have room for no more. With love, yours, Mummy."

I had some difficulty in persuading the Mother Superior to let me go after she had insisted on seeing my mother's letter, but as she was in as much of a quandary as I am myself, I think she was really glad that I firmly insisted on returning to Mummy however poor my welcome.

I can't believe it was only this morning that I said good-bye to the Convent. It seems months ago now since Mummy met me at the station. She gave me a kiss and said:

"Well, here's a pretty kettle of fish, Linda! And I hate your hat, dearie."

REFLECTION TWO

I can't sleep. The bed is too small for two people and Mummy is snoring so loudly that I know I shall never get a wink to-night.

I can't complain for there is not another corner in this house where one could put in a bed.

Bill is not bad and I think Mummy is wise to marry him. He is awfully fond of her, you can see that at once; he gives her an affectionate slap on the behind every time she goes near him.

I'm sure he's a good sort at heart, but, anyway, it is better for Mummy to be mistress of the "Cross Keys" than just "behind the bar".

I don't suppose husbands grow on gooseberry bushes, and Mummy is looking older these days. She has got fatter in the face and has put on a lot of weight since she broke her leg—that's her excuse, but I bet the number of ports she has with the customers has got something to do with it.

I can't help seeing how like Mummy I am in some ways. She has big grey eyes and a tiny turned-up nose which is now almost lost in her face since she has got fat.

One thing I've got which Mummy hasn't, and that is awfully good feet and hands.

Of course, I have been living in luxury the last few years while Mummy has been working, but that has nothing to do with the shape, and I'm glad I have long thin fingers and lovely nails.

The father of one of the girls at the Convent, who was a Doctor, said that good hands and feet are a sign of breeding, so perhaps mine come from my father, whoever he was.

I tried to have a talk with Mummy to-night before we came to bed, but I didn't get much opportunity, and she was tired when we got upstairs. But as I was undressing she did say:

"You know you are pretty, Linda, and if you weren't so thin you'd be even prettier—not but that it isn't fashionable nowadays to look like a lamp-post—though I must say all the men I've ever known like a curve or two, especially on the bust, and on the bustle."

"Especially Bill!" I said slyly, and Mummy laughed.

"Oh, Bill's a caution. Do you like him, dearie?"

"Yes," I said—and I meant it.

"He's reliable," Mummy said, "and, mind you, he has got a good bit put by. He's clever you know—but a bit close. Not that I am saying anything against him, mark you, but of course I got used to Alfred who never could save twopence. If Bill is close it's because he has to be. After all he has managed to buy this business out of his savings."

Although I didn't tell Mummy so I think Bill is mean. He has let out every room over the pub, and I know he is looking forward to the time when he and Mummy share one room and he can let the other.

I saw at once that it was quite useless to hope that he would let me stay until I get a job.

They are getting married the day after to-morrow, and Bill is looking for a tenant to come in that very evening to take possession of the vacant bedroom.

But what Mummy said to-night made me think. I wonder if there is any hope for me on the stage? After all, if you are pretty that is surely half the battle and I have always had rather a hankering after the boards—memories of the old days, I suppose.

Acting was one thing I could do well at the Convent, even though it was not encouraged.

But when we used to do a Shakespearean play once a year for the governors I always had the name part, and because I was good, the Nun who taught elocution took extra care over me.

I shall try to get a job to-morrow. I suppose Mummy has got a little money she could lend me until I earn some.

Poor old Mummy, if she goes on snoring like this when she is married I should think Bill will be sorry he has let that extra room.

REFLECTION THREE

I am absolutely dead beat, what with two days looking for work and the wedding yesterday, I am so tired I can hardly stand.

I have got a room for to-night in the house of Bill's cousin.

It is not very comfortable and from what I saw of the sheets it strikes me they have not been washed for some time, but it's better than nothing, and she is only charging me two shillings.

The wedding was a most exhausting business, but Mummy enjoyed herself and so did Bill.

She was married in blue velvet and she carried a huge bouquet of pink carnations. I couldn't be a bridesmaid, though I offered to be, because no one would buy me a new dress and my Convent clothes are dark blue, not exactly suitable for a bridesmaid!

Bill was beaming, and he wore a white button-hole as large as a cabbage, and the car they hired for the occasion was covered in white ribbons and orange blossom.

When they got back to the "Cross Keys" it was after three o'clock, and the public bar was closed for the afternoon, so we all celebrated in there until it was time to open again.

Bill will have to economise for years, I should think, to pay for all that was consumed during the afternoon and evening.

It was very late before we left the happy couple alone, and Bill's sister took me home and let me sleep on the sofa in her parlour. That was terribly uncomfortable and I am glad that to-night I can go to Bill's cousin.

Bill's relations have been awfully nice to me and Mummy has given me a "fiver" until I find myself some sort of a job.

But, oh, it is difficult! I went to all the agencies the day before yesterday and tried two or three theatres where they were having auditions, but they were all full up before I arrived.

In one of the agencies there was a little Jew man and he said:

"What do you want to do — what sort of part?" and when I said "Comic," he laughed like anything and said:

"Have you looked at your face?"

"Yes," I said, rather surprised, and he said:

"What you want is *ingenue* — you couldn't be comic if you tried with those eyes."

After that he tried to kiss me and it so annoyed me.

I dug my elbow as sharply as I could into his waist as he came near me, and he cried:

"Oh, you little bitch!"

But by that time I had reached the door and went out slamming it.

So that is one agent off the list!

I walked down Shaftesbury Avenue and the clothes were so lovely.

Mummy gave me one of her hats and I have altered it to fit me, but I could see at once that my school clothes are all wrong and quite hopeless.

It is only that I daren't spend much money yet.

I was so hungry when I came into this restaurant I had to order some sausages and mash even though I really meant to have something cheap before going back for the night.

I felt quite faint with hunger, and sausages and mash were a whole 1/2d, but there it is!

I feel lots better now I have had the sausages and mash, but I could eat the plateful all over again. It's funny I am so thin because I have a very good appetite really.

Even Bill said when I dined with him and Mummy:

"Linda has got hollow legs, I can't think where else she puts her food."

Oh, well, I suppose I must be getting off home.

I can't sit here all night, and the best thing is to get some sleep before I start looking for work again in the morning.

Look at those chocolate buns . . . I would love one . . . oozing with cream . . . I must have one!

REFLECTION FOUR

If things go on like this I shall begin to think my name is "Lucky Linda".

Really it seems that Mummy was right and that I was born under a lucky star. Here I am getting £3 a week in the chorus of *Whoops, dearie!* and all through getting to know Bessie!

If I had got up and gone as I intended after the sausages and mash that night I should have missed all this, it just shows that greed is sometimes rewarded.

I couldn't resist the chocolate cream bun I saw on the counter, and when I was tucking into it guiltily Bessie came in and ordered herself a steak and onions.

I liked her the moment I saw her, she has got such a jolly face, and when she smiled at me and said:

"Are you slimming?" of course I smiled back, and we got into conversation.

She has been in the chorus for years and knows all the ropes, and when I told her my troubles she was perfectly charming and the end of it was that here I am sharing a room with her in a funny little street off Tottenham Court Road.

She got me into *Whoops, dearie!* because, as she explained with a wink, the Assistant Stage Manager was after her and prepared to pay for it—up to a point!

I don't think it is much of a show myself, but, of course, I am no judge, not having been to theatres since I was eleven, but Bessie agrees with me it won't last long. I only hope we are wrong, for we are on clover while it does.

Bessie took me to a little second-hand clothes shop and I got a frightfully smart dress and coat for £3 — "blewing" my first week's wages, but I've still got some of Mummy's money in hand.

I didn't know enough about dancing to get into the dancing troupe with Bessie, but they have made me one of the Show-Girls.

I walk about the stage in the most lovely frocks and huge picture hats. They suit me and I would like to own a few of them for myself.

The leading lady looks a hundred when she is not made up. She used to be a well-known West End star, but she has come down in the world. She is kind though and not a bit catty or jealous.

The rehearsals were pretty strenuous. They kept us at the theatre until long after midnight, and I felt dead in the mornings, but now we've opened it's not so bad.

The second lead, a girl who dances quite well, but who can't sing for toffee, gets very temperamental, and when she bursts into tears, has to be smoothed down by everyone.

The dresses we wear are all made by a male dress designer, and he keeps tearing in and making alterations, and when I appeared he said to the Producer:

"Stop! Stop! It is too devastating. I particularly said that red model was to be worn by a brunette, and now they have given it an *absolute* blonde."

Everyone turned to look at me, and, personally, I thought the red dress looked lovely, but, of course, I couldn't say so, and only after a terrific argument the young designer agreed that it would have to be left on me, as it was too tight for the other Show-Girls.

But in the wings he went on murmuring for ages afterwards:

"It's *too* infuriating! Really, theatrical production makes me weep."

26

I was terrified that I would lose my job, but Bessie told me not to take any notice, as she had been in a show he dressed before, and that he always behaved like that.

"Is he a success?" I asked.

"He makes millions," she answered, "as it's the fashion now to have men designers of women's clothes! That's why they insist on making all their models for flat-chested girls with no hips. Pansy-ish, if you ask me. It's all right for you, Linda, but I daren't eat a thing now until the show is over."

I am tired to-night, and I ought to be asleep if I don't want to look a freak to-morrow for the *matinee*, but I've got to mend these stockings—bother holes and runs!

I'm not really complaining, it is all so exciting—!

REFLECTION FIVE

I am frightfully thrilled because I am going out to-night for the first time.

Bessie is taking me with her and her boy. She has a regular one now ever since the show started.

Bessie calls him a "boy", but that is just a manner of speaking, for he is quite old—thirty-five at least and awfully clever, at least Bessie says so; he is in a stock-broking firm in the city.

He has a wife, too, and that would put me off if I was Bessie. I always feel that married men belong to someone else.

But Bessie doesn't care. In fact, I am surprised in some ways how little Bessie does care about anything.

She likes Teddy, as she calls him, and when he is with us, makes ever such a fuss of him. But when he is not there she never talks about him or seems to mind one way or another, except when he sends her presents.

I asked her one day if she was jealous of his wife, and she answered:

"What questions you do ask, Linda! Is it likely? My dear, she is very much the grand lady of Walton Health. She and I won't come to blows over Teddy, I can assure you."

"I can't understand it, Bessie," I said, "because if I were you I should mind."

Bessie has been away with him two or three week-ends, and I know she often goes back to his flat after the show.

She comes in ever so late—or rather ever so early— waking me up, though not for long for she just drags off her clothes and simply flops into bed.

I have never had much to say to Teddy, just: "How do you do?" when he has come round to the stage door for Bessie, or stood outside the dressing-room waiting for her.

But, to-night Teddy is bringing a friend along to meet me, and it is all rather exciting because apparently the friend has seen me from the front, and he told Teddy that he thought I was lovely, and so of course, after that, a meeting had to be arranged.

I have got a marvellous dress, it is pale blue tulle, and it belonged to some rich girl who had only worn it two or three times and then her maid sold it to the shop—at least that is what the woman told me at the Dress Agency.

Anyway, it only wanted the tiniest bit of alteration which I could do myself, and it really does make my hair look nice.

I went to a little shop in Wardour Street and I have had my hair curled all up the back of my head, and if Teddy's friend thought I looked nice on the stage I shall be furious if he doesn't think I look a thousand times better off.

Not all the girls have boys by any means, in fact it surprised me how few of them do. Most of them hurry home by themselves when the show is over, and it is only the leading lady who comes in a car.

I am awfully excited to see what my first admirer will be like.

Bessie says his name is Tony Haywood and that he is a member of Teddy's Club, otherwise she doesn't know anything about him.

I do hope he thinks I am pretty, especially in my new dress.

Then, perhaps, he will take me out lots of times and I shall have "a regular boy" like Bessie.

REFLECTION SIX

I am so excited I can't sleep, but I don't mind.

I want to lie awake for hours thinking about the lovely evening we have had.

Bessie is not home yet, and I don't expect she will be until nearly morning, so I am all alone in the room, and when I was undressing I danced around, the tunes of the band going on and on in my head.

We went to the Savoy; it was quite the most exciting place I have ever seen, and it was simply packed with people.

Teddy was apparently well known as they bowed him in and we had a very good table near the floor.

I was secretly rather shy of it all, so that I could hardly pay any attention at first to Tony Haywood.

When I did have a proper look at him I was just a tiny bit disappointed because he was not very tall, dark, with a chin which had a sort of bluey look, as if he could not shave close enough.

However, he was very nice and quite amusing, and made Bessie and Teddy laugh a lot.

"This is Linda's first night out in London," Bessie announced.

Then they all drank my health and I had champagne for the first time. It is not bad, although I'm not sure I didn't prefer the port we had at Mummy's wedding.

But perhaps champagne is better for a party because it is all fizzy and exciting, and in a way expresses the bubbling-over feeling one has at a party.

I can't quite put it into words, but the whole evening seemed rather like champagne. I felt quite breathless about it all, and all the time I was terrified I should miss something.

And I think I must have looked nice because I saw two men look at me when I was dancing; and one said:

"There's something new. What do you think of that, old boy?"

Tony said all sorts of complimentary and nice things, and I hope he was being truthful. He danced very well, too. I was a bit nervous at first in case I wasn't good enough, but we got along all right.

I danced once with Teddy, but he was rather queer. I didn't like it very much, he held me very tight and he said:

"Have you got a lot of young men, Linda? Bessie says you haven't, but I don't believe her."

"No, I haven't," I answered, "because I have only just come to London."

"You won't be long without them, I promise you that, my dear," he said.

He gave me a sort of squeeze.

I pretended not to notice and replied casually:

"I hope you are right."

"Do you really mean that?" he whispered in my ear. "If I thought . . ."

He gave me a funny sort of look and held me closer still, so that I almost screamed because he hurt.

Luckily at that moment Bessie came dancing by with Tony, and she called out:

"Come on, Teddy, you mustn't monopolise Linda, Tony wants to dance with her again."

So we changed partners in the middle of the room, and I must say I wasn't sorry, because I don't like Teddy very much; perhaps it is because he is so much older.

We had the most delicious things to eat for supper, but I was so excited that I could hardly eat anything—even

31

though I knew that to-morrow I would be sorry I didn't.

I was enjoying myself too much to want to go home, but Bessie kept fussing round Teddy and saying she thought we ought to go.

I don't really believe he wanted to, but she insisted, and when we all got out into the hall, she turned to Tony and said:

"You will take Linda home, won't you? I will go with Teddy."

So we got into separate taxis. We drove for a minute or two in silence, and then Tony put out his hand and took mine and asked:

"Have you enjoyed yourself to-night?"

"So much," I answered, "I can't believe it is true."

Tony looked at me for a second in such a funny way, then he said:

"Don't get spoilt too quickly."

I didn't know what to say to that, so I looked at him and murmured:

"I don't suppose I shall have much opportunity."

"I am quite certain you will," he replied rather dryly, as if he wasn't awfully pleased about it.

"I wish to heaven I hadn't come to-night," he said.

"Oh, why?" I asked, terribly upset, of course.

"It's a long story," Tony answered, "and I am not going to tell you now. Will you come and have supper with me to-morrow night, somewhere quiet, where we can talk?"

Of course, I replied that I would like to and he said:

"All right, I will come for you after the show."

"Shall we take Teddy and Bessie?" I asked.

Again he looked at me in a funny sort of way before he said:

"Is Bessie a friend of yours?"

"Of course, my very best friend. I can't tell you how kind she has been."

"Well, if you want to be kind to her," said Tony, "I should not see too much of her young man."

"Teddy?" I questioned.

"Exactly!" was the answer.

At that moment we got home. Tony got out and said:

"Good night, Linda! I will see you to-morrow."

And he drove away before I could thank him for the

evening. It is all rather muddling and exciting, and I wish I knew what he meant about Teddy.

He couldn't have meant that Teddy liked me too much, because, after all, I know he is devoted to Bessie and gives her the most lovely presents. He gave her a silver fox fur only last week.

Bessie has known him for a long time, too, although they didn't see so much of each other until the beginning of last month.

Anyway, I don't like Teddy, but I like Tony, although he is not a bit the sort of person I should ever fall in love with. But if he will take me out and give me a good time, that will be absolutely marvellous.

I am glad he didn't try to kiss me, as I was rather afraid he might. Which reminds me, to-morrow I must find out what he meant by being sorry he had come.

I think I hear Bessie's step on the stairs. She is early, but I will pretend to be asleep, even though I am longing to talk to her.

She is often so cross when she comes home from seeing Teddy, it is wisest not to talk . . .

Yes, it is Bessie.

REFLECTION SEVEN

The most awful thing has happened and I simply can't believe it.

When I woke up this morning Bessie was still asleep and I got up and got her breakfast as I often do, and took her in a cup of tea when she woke.

I thought she was a bit queer. But she is never very gossipy first thing in the morning, so I didn't take much notice.

About eleven o'clock there came a bang at the door and a messenger boy with a lot of flowers and a note, and he said:

"Miss Linda Snell?"

"Yes, that's me," I said, absolutely thrilled with the flowers.

I called Bessie to look at them and said:

"Oh, look at my lovely flowers, Bessie. I suppose Tony must have sent them."

Then, to my horror, I caught sight of the card. They were not from Tony at all, they were from Teddy, and the note said:

"Here's to wish you good morning and can you lunch

*with me to-day? Savoy Grill at 1 o'clock. Do come
and give the boy your message, but mind it is Yes.
Yours, Teddy."*

When I read it I said:

"Oh, this can't be for me, this is for you, Bessie, and
passed it over to her.

She read it and then picked up the envelope, and there
was written as plain as anything "Miss Linda Snell".

Bessie didn't say a word but just threw the letter down
on the bed and walked over to the looking-glass and started
to comb her hair.

"But, Bessie," I cried, "I don't understand this."

"Oh, well, I do," she said.

"Bessie, it is so absurd—does he mean both of us?"

Then she turned on me in a fury and cried:

"No, he doesn't, Linda, and you know damned well he
doesn't, and all I can say is you might have kept your
hands off my boy."

I tried to expostulate and said:

"Bessie, don't you see . . ."

But she only answered:

"Go to hell!"

She slammed off into a corner, and even though I could-
n't see her face I knew she was very near to tears.

Then I picked up the flowers from my bed where I had
put them, and took them out to the boy and said:

"Take these to the gentleman and tell him I don't want
them, and the answer is 'no.'"

He looked a bit surprised, but he went off whistling.

Then I came back into the room, and after a moment
Bessie, who had heard all I had said, came across and put
her arms round me and said:

"You shouldn't have done that, Linda. It doesn't matter; I don't want him really, except that it's a bit trying
when your boy gets absolutely peeled off you."

"Bessie, I didn't mean to," I protested, "I had no idea,
honest injun."

"I know you didn't. It just happens sometimes like that.
You are so pretty, that is the trouble."

Then we sat and talked and I told her about Tony, and
she was awfully nice, but I could see that she was worried
about herself.

At one o'clock we went out to lunch together and had a couple of ham sandwiches and some coffee at a snack bar round the corner.

Bessie seemed a bit more cheerful after that and we went for a walk to look at the shops, and I said to her:

"But, Bessie, I don't understand, if Teddy loves you how can he possibly want to send me flowers all of a sudden like that?"

"My dear," she said, "if he is paying for it, he would just as soon have it tuppence coloured, and you are something new and much prettier than I ever was, even at your age. And as for love, Teddy is not in love with me; he is just the kind that likes to have a mistress so that he can swank among his friends in the City. There is the sort who talk and the sort who keep things very quiet, and you can take it from me that Teddy is the talking sort."

"But his friend Tony is quite different," I said, "he didn't even try to kiss me, last night."

"I am surprised at that," Bessie said, "he looks to me a bit of a pouncer. However, you will find out to-night."

"And if he tries to kiss me," I asked, "do you think I ought to let him?"

Bessie stopped dead in the middle of the street and stared at me.

Then she answered:

"Do you know, Linda, at times I think you are half-witted. I suppose it is being brought up in a Convent, but what you don't seem to realise is that your innocence is the most valuable thing you have got."

"That isn't saying much," I answered.

"Now listen to me," Bessie said seriously, taking my arm, "most men like something young, and they are prepared to pay for it. Don't you give them anything unless you have to. Don't kiss them, don't even let them hold your hand, until they have paid, and paid heavily for the privilege.

"My dear, do you suppose I don't know after years of messing about, having one boy after another keen on me, and always realising that the older I get the more I have got to give for the money, so to speak?"

"But I wasn't talking about living with anybody," I said.

"Well, what is the difference?" Bessie said. "If you are

36

going to kiss and mess about you might as well go the whole way and make an end of it. You take my advice, Linda, and let no one touch you."

She sighed.

"I expect like most of us you will fall in love before you know where you are, and give yourself away, body and soul, to somebody who doesn't appreciate it. But if you don't you might do anything with yourself.

"Why with your looks you ought to marry somebody rich and get settled for life. Security. That is what all of us want really at heart."

"I don't know that I am in a hurry to get married," I said.

"Take my advice," Bessie replied. "You keep yourself to yourself, Linda Snell, and you make your price a wedding ring, and mind it's a platinum one, too."

"You're a gold digger, Bessie," I said.

She laughed and replied:

"Of course I am, and what woman isn't? There are gold diggers in every class from the highest to the lowest. In the highest the little virgins sell themselves on the red carpet of St. Margaret's, Westminster, to the most eligible young man they can find, and nobody thinks anything about it. But if a poor girl has to feed herself and takes a fiver or so out of anyone they call her a gold digger.

"And as for men," Bessie went on, "they are all the same, making a song and dance if you don't give them their own way, and despising you when you do."

"The less you give a man the more he admires you. You give them nothing, Linda, and they will come around after you like rats after aniseed."

REFLECTION EIGHT

When it came to the point of going out with Tony Haywood last night and leaving Bessie to go home alone because she was not seeing Teddy at the theatre, I could hardly bear to do it.

I felt so ashamed. I begged her to come with us and Tony asked her, too, when he realised that she had no other invitation.

But she was just as obstinate as she could be.

"Two is company. Off you go and enjoy yourselves, and don't let Linda get into any mischief," she said to Tony.

"Not with me, anyway," he answered quite solemnly as if he was making her a promise.

We started off and, of course, I was wearing my blue dress again, but I had Bessie's evening coat of black velvet over it.

I had been awfully embarrassed at the Savoy because I had no evening coat and had to wear my day coat, which is cloth, and the woman in the cloakroom almost snorted when she took it.

However, I felt fine to-night, and I was quite disappointed when Tony took me to supper to quite a quiet little place instead of where I could be seen by lots of people.

But I was glad to have some really good food again, and he ordered a bottle of champagne without even asking me what I would like.

We were both a bit stiff at first and rather awkward, and then he asked me about Bessie, and I told him what had happened and he seemed awfully surprised, and said he couldn't understand Teddy behaving like that.

I told him that I had sent the flowers back, and he said that he thought it was marvellous of me to be so loyal to my friend.

"I didn't want them, anyway," I said, "if they came from him."

And Tony looked at me in a funny sort of way, and asked:

"Is that quite true, Linda?"

When I thought quite honestly about it, I don't know if it is. They were such lovely roses, and it seems to me that if one is absolutely truthful roses are roses whoever has given them to you.

So I admitted that perhaps it wasn't quite true, and that I would have liked to have kept them if that hadn't been the only way that I could show both him and Bessie that I wasn't prepared to be friends with him.

"I nearly sent you some flowers to-day, Linda," Tony said. "I wish I had now. Then I thought that perhaps you would rather have this instead."

He produced, from under his arm, a little flat box he had been carrying, and when I opened it there was the most lovely evening bag made in gold brocade with a funny coloured stone clasp.

Of course I was absolutely thrilled.

"Well, there you are," he said. "You will find it more useful than flowers, which die in a day or two, and it's a present entirely without prejudice."

I asked what he meant by "without prejudice".

"It means you haven't got to be too grateful," he answered laughing.

"But I can't help being grateful," I said. "I think it is the most lovely thing I have ever had in my life."

"I didn't exactly mean that," he answered; "but never mind, Linda, I am so glad you like it."

Then all the delicious things he had ordered came and I couldn't attend much to Tony until I had finished them.

Afterwards there was coffee, and he said without looking at me:

"I am not going to ask you out again, Linda."

"Oh, why?" I said frightfully disappointed.

"Because I am going to be married," he answered.

"I am sorry," I answered without thinking, but then I blushed and amended it by adding: "I mean I am awfully glad for you, but I am sorry I am not going to see you again. Would your fiancée be jealous of me?"

"Have you ever looked at yourself in the glass, Linda?" he asked very quietly.

"Of course I have," I replied, and he said:

"Well, now you know, and I don't suppose you will ever be much of a success where women are concerned."

"Are you awfully in love?" I asked.

Tony hesitated for just a moment before he answered, and then he asked:

"Do you want to know the truth?"

"Yes," I replied, "I always think it is so tiresome if one doesn't tell the truth about things. If you have to pretend you might as well not say anything."

Tony laughed at that and said:

"Dear Linda, what a politician you would make."

Then serious again he went on:

"You see, Linda, my fiancée's father is head of my firm and a very important man. I have seen a lot of his daughter Helen, and we get on very well together, and I even thought I was rather in love with her until . . . well, until something happened."

"What?" I said curiously.

When I asked that he stared at me and then looked away for a long time before he spoke, and when he did his voice was funny and quite hoarse.

"When I first saw you, Linda."

"Do you mean you fell in love with me?" I asked.

He nodded without speaking and took my hand under the table and squeezed it so hard that I thought he would break my fingers.

"Oh, Tony, I *am* sorry — and now I have spoilt your marriage!" I said.

Tony stared at me and started talking very quickly.

"It is absurd, absolutely absurd. Do you suppose I haven't told myself that over and over again. I had no idea anyone could want a person as much as I want you.

"It is madness to see you, madness to think about you, and do you suppose I don't know I am making a fool of myself? Even if I didn't marry Helen it wouldn't help matters.

"Do you know how much money I have got of my own? A few hundreds a year. Not enough for you, Linda, my beautiful, and not enough for me."

He stopped speaking as suddenly as he had started, beckoned the waiter and told him to bring him some brandy.

We sat silent until it came, as there didn't seem to be anything I could say although I was awfully sorry about it all.

After a few moments Tony seemed calmer, and then he said:

"There is only one thing I can do for you, Linda, and that is get you out of that frightful second-rate show you are in now. You can do much better for yourself than that."

"But I was thrilled to get it," I answered. "If you only knew how difficult it is to get a job in any show. I walked around for days to the agencies and they wouldn't even look at me."

"My dear," he said, "the stage is not the right life for you."

"But it is, I am sure it is," I protested. "Not what I am doing now, being a show girl. I don't want to do that a bit, I want a comic part — I do really!"

Tony laughed.

"It is amazing, absolutely amazing how incredibly stupid people are about themselves," he said. "How could you with your looks possibly think that you could ever do anything comic? No! What I suggest for you is that you become a mannequin at one of the big model houses.

"It's a much better life, much better pay, and you have got much more chance of meeting people who will take you out to parties and things. Not that I particularly want to think of that aspect of it."

"Mannequin work," I said. "Does that mean showing off clothes all day? Why, that sounds a very easy job to me."

"It's not as easy as you think," Tony answered, "but

41

I can fix it for you, I feel sure, because my business is wholesale materials and I happen to know the managers of two or three well-known dress houses, and as they are always grumbling about their models I should think they would absolutely jump at you.

"Anyway, it is a better life than kicking about with that awful crowd. You must see that that show of yours is ghastly. And you are never likely to meet anyone except men who are already 'fixed up' with some girl, like Edward."

"It would be too marvellous if I could get a better job," I said.

Really what an opportunity this would be if Tony could fix it for me.

"I will do that to-morrow," Tony said, "and I expect it will be the last thing I will be able to do for you, Linda."

And after that the evening got rather sad and tragic, and then we got into a taxi and Tony sat grimly in his corner looking absolutely miserable. As we got nearly back to my street I said:

"Tony, I do want to thank you for the lovely bag and for being so awfully kind to me. Bessie said I oughtn't to, but I don't care, and if you would like to kiss me, I should like you to."

And Tony gave me a sort of funny cry and put his arms round me and held me very tight, but he didn't kiss me.

He only put his face against mine, terribly close, for a long minute and then he said: "Oh, God!" in a funny strangled sort of voice.

The taxi stopped and he got out at once almost hurriedly as if he was glad we had arrived.

"Good-bye, Linda!" he said.

Before I could get my latch-key into the door he had jumped back into the taxi and had driven away.

I don't know why, but I felt awfully, awfully sad and even my lovely new bag didn't make me feel completely happy about the evening.

REFLECTION NINE

I can't believe I have been here a week and yet at the same time I am beginning to feel as if it were months, even years, since I left the Convent, since Mummy's wedding, and since I tramped the streets thinking I should never find a job of any sort.

I feel very rich to be earning four pounds a week and a guinea extra every time I do special photographs or other shows. But I find I have a lot of extras, too. My hair, for instance.

I didn't see Tony again but only got a letter from him, very brief and just telling me to call on Mr. Cantaloupe in Bond Street.

Bessie was absolutely thrilled when she heard the name, because apparently Mr. Cantaloupe is the most important dress designer of the moment, not only in London, but also in Paris.

Anyway, the shop is certainly impressive enough, and the most majestic butler flung open the door when I arrived and gave me an awful look as if he realised everything about me was wrong, which I now know was quite true.

I told him I had an appointment and was led along the

corridor covered with the thickest and most scrunchy blue carpet to an office at the back.

There was a desk and a girl in grey typing, who said: "Mr. Cantaloupe will see you in a few moments, sit down, please."

So I sat down feeling rather like a kitchen-maid applying for a new situation, because I realised that I could never aspire to move about in a magnificent house like this.

The telephone kept ringing and the very refined typist kept saying into the house 'phone: "The Duchess of Wrexboro' wishes to alter her appointment from Tuesday at three o'clock to Thursday at four. Will that be all right?" Or else she replied: "No, I am afraid Mr. Cantaloupe can see no one to-morrow, he is flying to Paris to-night."

She was so frightfully grand and inhuman that I felt quite relieved when, as a call came through, she gave a quick glance at me, decided I didn't matter, then said:

"Oh, all right, Annie, tell mother I'll come right back. I was going to the pictures, but tell her I'll be back at seven o'clock at the very latest."

Then, in another moment she was doing her superior stuff again:

"Oh, yes, Mr. Cantaloupe will be delighted to see Lady Engledene. Yes, yes, he is keeping a special time for her."

And then a buzzer went and she got up and said to me: "This way, please," and led me into the other room.

And there was a very thin man, quite young, with long artistic fingers, and he held a book of patterns in one hand and a cigarette in a long black onyx holder in the other.

There were two girls with him, and one was dressed in the most lovely dress of silver and the other one was in grey like the typist.

As I came in he said to the girl in silver:

"It's too terrible. Take it to the workroom at once and tell them to take it completely to bits."

When the girl in silver had disappeared behind the blue curtains which hid half the room, the girl in grey said, looking at me:

"This is the model Mr. Haywood wrote to you about, and we are short of blondes at the moment, you know."

"Yes, yes!" Mr. Cantaloupe answered, and addressing me, he said:

"Take off your hat and coat."

44

I did as I was told and he looked at me for a long time and then walked all round me looking at my feet, ankles and hands, and scrutinising me so intently that I expected at any moment that he would look at my teeth as I have seen people do to horses.

At last he spoke, and he said:

"Who does your hair? It is too terrible, you must have it seen to at once. Go to François and tell him I sent you. He must find an individual style, of course."

"What is your name?"

"Linda Snell," I replied.

"Dear, dear!" he exclaimed. "We must try to forget the last part. Linda is not so bad, it might have been worse."

Then he said to the girl in grey: "See to it," and she walked across the room and opened the door and I picked up my hat and coat and followed her.

Outside I said:

"Does this mean I am engaged?"

"Of course!"

Then she told me I was to have four pounds a week and I nearly fainted with surprise. I had no idea that mannequins were so highly paid.

I went off to François at once and he also ejaculated and screamed about my hair until I felt I had committed some awful crime having my hair curled.

He arranged it absolutely flat on my head with only a few curls at my ears and just one row across the back, and it comes low across my forehead with hardly any wave.

I felt quite queer when he had finished, but I must say it is very becoming and makes me look quite different.

But if Mr. Cantaloupe was frightening, it was not half as bad as meeting the girls the next morning.

When I entered the mannequin's room they were all sitting about either in the most wonderful lace cami-knickers, or else in silk wrappers provided by the house.

They were talking among themselves in a sort of languid way, and I felt as I felt that first day at the Convent years ago, as if I were a complete outsider and would never be allowed to join in with the others.

But now after a week I have learnt that their manner is because they are so tired, and most of them daren't have enough to eat even if they can afford it in case they put on any more weight.

45

Mr. Cantaloupe won't employ anyone who has even an extra inch on their hips.

They are all mad with envy that I can eat so much and not show it, and most of their conversation is of diets and how to get their weight down another pound or two.

Cleone is much the prettiest there. She is dark, with very short hair curled like a Grecian statue round her head.

She is a Countess, too, although only an Italian one, and has not seen her husband for five years, and although she calls herself the Countess di Rivoli apparently it is very doubtful whether he is married to her at all.

He came over here to buy balloons for the Italian Government five years ago and stayed three months longer than he ought to have done to marry Cleone.

Then he went back to Italy and she has never heard from him since.

Apparently that doesn't worry her very much for she is a tremendous success and lunches nearly every day at the Ritz.

She goes out every night to all sorts of exciting parties and meets all the people who appear week by week in what the girls call the "snob press"—which means the *Tatler*, the *Sketch* and the *Bystander*.

It is awfully exciting to see the customers after one has read about them being at the races or attending a Ball.

To-day Lady Marigold Carstairs came in, and the girls all had lots to tell me about her, so that I peeped through the curtains just in case she didn't want to see any of the dresses I wore.

Apparently she is quite notorious, gives the most amazing parties in London and asks all sorts of people.

She has had three husbands already although she is only thirty-two and is having a great *affaire* with one of the biggest newspaper men in the country.

He was not with her, but two other men, one whom the girls said they called "Tiny" Spencer because he was so big.

Lord Glaxly looked to me rather a stupid young man with a receding chin and a very pink and white complexion.

The girls told me that he was known as "Pimples" because when he was younger he had spots which showed so frightfully on his face.

Lady Marigold and the two young men kept roaring with laughter all the time, and it seemed as if she wasn't paying any attention to the dresses.

But she must have been really because she had chosen two even before her *vendeuse*, Madame Jean, told me to put on the white tulle model and show it.

Although I have put on hundreds of dresses during the last week it always gives me a thrill every time I do so, because they are so lovely.

I can hardly believe that I thought the blue tulle I wore at the Savoy that night was smart.

Cantaloupe's models have wonderful lines and are quite plain and yet make one look very dressed up.

I walked in to show it and walked round swaying from the hips as the girls had shown me how to, and then I heard Lord Glaxly say: "That's a pretty girl!"

And Lady Marigold turned to Madame Jean and said: "You have a new mannequin—who is she?"

I heard Madame Jean say my name as I walked back behind the black velvet curtains, and in a moment the message came through that I was to put on the green lace.

When I was dressed and parted the curtains I heard Lady Marigold say:

"All right, Pimples, leave it to me, don't fuss!"

When I had shown the dress she said to Madame Jean:

"I really can't decide—would you be good enough to send the white and the green up to-night at six o'clock and I will try them on? Or what is better still, send the mannequin with them and she can put them on for me; I really can't stop now."

Madame Jean replied:

"That will be quite all right. I will see to that, My Lady."

"Thanks so much," Lady Marigold answered, then turning to me she said: "You will come along at six then, with the dresses?"

I said I would, and they all swept out. When they had gone Madame Jean said:

"You have had a success."

"Have I, who with?" I asked.

47

"Lady Marigold's brother—that is why they want you to go up to-night," she replied.

"They don't really want to see the dresses then," I said. "Do you think I had better not go?"

"You will do as you are told," Madame Jean answered, "and don't be a little fool—enjoy yourself while you get the chance. Why, you can meet everyone in London at Allwood House."

So after that I was in a perfect flutter all the afternoon, and the girls kept telling me things about Lady Marigold and how she eloped when she was seventeen with her father's secretary who was years older than she.

She ran away from him two years later with an explorer, and then married Sir Arthur Carstairs, but they are going to have a divorce at any moment.

It is funny, because she is not exactly pretty—fascinating, and, of course, wonderfully dressed and turned out, but one has to have more than looks, I've discovered — it's personality.

I am terrified that mine won't be good enough and I shall lose my job, because four days after I arrived the most lovely girl got the sack. She was dark and awfully pretty, though she wasn't exactly chic.

I asked the girls about her when she left and they said she was an absolute flop, and for some reason nobody ever bought the dresses she wore.

She was not a success anywhere either in the shop or out, and that was no use to Cantaloupe, who likes his girls not only to sell dresses, but also to be seen everywhere.

"But, why do you think he has taken me? Because I don't know *anyone*," I asked.

And Cleone said:

"You are a dark horse, Linda. You are all right, the money is five to four on you at the moment."

I can't help being a bit excited about going to Lady Marigold's, even though I am afraid I shall not know how to behave, and I tried to ask Cleone just now what I should do and she said:

"Just be yourself, Linda. You will learn soon enough without instruction."

And one of the girls passed us while we were talking and asked:

"Do you think Linda is another Star? We haven't had a really spectacular one since Molly married the Marquis."

"Linda may be a star," Cleone answered, "who knows, but you wouldn't call "Pimples" one of the wise men, would you?"

At that they all laughed.

REFLECTION TEN

I shall have to move into other rooms, I can see that.

The only bathroom in our lodgings was engaged for over twenty minutes this morning and I am late for work and Madame Jean is sure to be annoyed when I arrive.

I like to walk too, but here I am on top of a bus instead of getting some fresh air. I feel awfully shut up, spending all day in Cantaloupe's.

I suppose I am still used to the strong northern air, and the amount of exercise we got at the Convent playing games.

At the shop there is always a sickly smell of scent, not only from Cantaloupe's own bottles which he sells at exorbitant prices, but also from the customers who seem at times to absolutely pour it over themselves.

Yet, if I am honest, it is not only because of the bathroom that I want to leave my lodgings, it's also because of Bessie.

I know it is beastly of me to say it and I feel ashamed of myself for finding fault with her after she has been such a jolly good friend to me.

If it hadn't been for her I would never be in the good job I am, and having this good time, but since I left the

50

show she has been different, sort of disagreeable and sarcastic about everything I do.

It is bad enough having nobody to tell things to without actually sleeping in the same room with someone who is resentful.

Last night was about the limit, for I got in only a few minutes after Bessie, and no one had taken her out although, I understand, she and Teddy have patched up things since I left.

She came back from the theatre quite untired and in the old days would have been ready for anything. But when I tore upstairs and into the room saying:

"Bessie, what do you think has happened to me?" she was grumpy and not a bit interested in Lady Marigold's party.

I suppose Bessie is a bit jealous if the truth was told, and, horrid though it may be of me, I do see that compared with the girls at Cantaloupe's she is awfully bad style.

I know that I would be ashamed for them to see me with her, and that is a terrible thing for me to think, and just shows what a cheap horrid person I must be.

I know one ought to be able to stick to one's friends through thick and thin whatever they are like.

But if poor Bessie compares badly with the girls at Cantaloupe's, I know she would seem absolutely terrible beside Lady Marigold and her set.

And the funny thing is that it is not because Bessie has got dyed hair and is very made up or anything like that, because Lady Marigold's friends are absolutely sensational —or is flamboyant the right word?—compared with any chorus girl I have ever seen.

Why, one woman at her party, who is Princess something or other, although she is an American, had black fingernails and a lipstick the color of blackberries.

However, when I got to Lady Marigold's I wasn't concerned by their looks, I was taken up to her bedroom first of all and told to unpack the dresses, which I did, being helped by her maid who was French and awfully superior and condescending.

I have never seen anything like Lady Marigold's bedroom.

All the furniture was silver and looking-glass, and the

51

bed was orange velvet with a huge tiger-skin cover over it —most awfully weird. The ceiling was gold and orange glass all put together like mosaic.

And while I was looking at the room and deciding that it was too queer for anything I should like to have, the door opened and Lady Marigold came in.

She had a cocktail in one hand and a cigarette in the other and she said:

"Oh, you have brought the dresses, have you? That is marvellous, but I can't see them for a moment, so will you come down and have a cocktail until I can."

As I said: "Thank you very much," Lord Glaxly's face came peeping around the door. When he saw me he stared and then he said:

"Can I come in, Marigold?"

She laughed.

"You are impatient, Pimples. Why didn't you wait downstairs as I told you? Well, all right, as you are here—come in!"

Turning to me she said:

"This is my brother."

We shook hands and I felt quite silly because I saw that Lady Marigold was not the slightest bit interested in the dresses.

"Come on, let's go downstairs to the others," she said, and I followed her.

We went into a huge room with absolutely hundreds of people, all chattering and laughing and drinking cocktails, the place was thick with smoke, and they seemed to be making an extraordinary high-pitched chattering noise.

"Will you have a cocktail?" Lord Glaxly asked: and brought me one.

I squeezed myself into a corner by a table and tried to talk to him, but I found it awfully difficult as the noise was awful.

People kept moving past us and shouting: "Hello, Pimples, how are you?" but not waiting for an answer, just drifting away again.

Then the other man who had been at the dress show came up and shook me by the hand without waiting to be introduced, and said:

"You did look topping this afternoon in those dresses. Do you like that sort of thing?"

I replied that I did, and he said:

"Well, it is all right for women, but you and I wouldn't cut much of a figure as mannequins, eh, Pimples?"

While they were talking another man came up. He was tall and rather nice-looking, but much older, at least forty-five, and he said:

"I want to be introduced."

"Tiny", the one who had come to the dress show answered:

"Nonsense, Peter, you go away. Vera is looking for you somewhere!"

But the new man turned to me and said:

"Well, if they won't introduce me, I shall have to do it myself. I know your name because Marigold has just told me. It's Linda, isn't it?"

"Linda Snell," I answered, and he said:

"Oh, Linda is good enough for me. I won't bother about the other part, mine is Peter."

He elbowed his way next to me and talked away and was really most awfully interesting.

He asked me what I had done and what I had seen in London, and when I told him I had been nowhere except the Savoy he was horrified and said that must be remedied at once, and he would see to it.

He told me that I was the prettiest girl he had seen for ages, and he said it in such a way that I could only laugh and say:

"Thank you!"

"What are you doing this evening?" he asked.

Before I could answer, Lord Glaxly, who was listening said:

"She is dining with me."

I suppose I looked surprised for this was the first time I had heard of it, although, of course, he may have asked me in all the noise when I couldn't hear what he was saying.

"All right, Pimples, we will all go together; Peter said: "you had better enjoy your innings while you have the chance."

At that Lord Glaxly looked quite sulky, but he didn't say anything, and Peter went on talking to me.

While he was telling me a story, a little thin, fair-haired woman came up to us. She was pretty in a discontented, rather catty sort of way, but she made one think of something feline and rather treacherous.

"Peter," she said, "I have been looking for you everywhere, we have got to go on to the Lawson's now."

"Sorry, old girl," Peter answered, "but I can't come. I have promised Marigold I would see this party out and dine with her."

The cat-woman was absolutely furious.

"I have never heard such nonsense," she said. "You promised to take me to the Lawson's and I wanted you to come to the Hope's reception to-night."

"Sorry, I can't manage it," Peter answered indifferently.

Then the cat-woman looked at me with a sort of withering look and back again at Peter.

"Crèche work again, Peter," she said, "if you choose them much younger you will be there before the midwife!"

With that she walked away.

Peter hesitated a moment, then he said:

"Don't go, will you, I will be back again in a moment," and hurried after her.

When he had gone I said to Lord Glaxly:

"Who is that?"

"Which?" he asked.

"Both," I replied.

"Peter is Rantoun," he said. "You know who I mean."

When I replied that I didn't he explained that he was the Earl of Rantoun and was always about everywhere.

"What does he do?" I asked.

"Oh, nothing much—gives other people's wives a good time and toddles into the Lords occasionally," Lord Glaxly answered.

"And Vera?" I questioned.

"Oh, she has lasted a long time," he replied, "quite six months. They were due for a bust-up, anyway. But, look here, you are not to let him monopolise you. He will try to, of course, he always does with anyone new and pretty. You promise that, don't you?"

"I don't think that is at all likely," I said lamely, rather hoping he would.

"Oh, yes it is," Lord Glaxly assured me, "he will give you a rush, and none of us will see you for dust. He is awfully rich, you see, and the girls like him."

I could understand women liking Peter far better than

54

Lord Glaxly, who I was finding most terribly difficult to talk to. Peter makes one laugh, and thoughts come absolutely bubbling out of one.

But I was sorry for Pimples. To begin with, what an awful name to be called. He is limp somehow, the sort of person who would never stand up for himself.

I tried to be nice to him, but I must say that I was glad when Peter returned to us again.

People were beginning to go and I kept looking anxiously at Lady Marigold in case she wanted me, but she was deep in conversation and didn't even look in my direction.

A few moments later the butler announced:

"Mr. Arthur Unwin."

A very nice-looking tall young man came hurrying into the room.

"Marigold, darling, I can't apologise enough, but I have had the most abortive day and couldn't get here before."

Lady Marigold was obviously delighted to see him and they talked together for a few moments, and then she turned to us and said:

"Arthur wants me to dine with him, so I can't come with you, Peter, but you take Miss Snell, and Pimples can go along as chaperon!"

She laughed mischievously as if she knew that neither of them would care for that situation.

"Thank you very much," I said, "but I think I had better be getting along home."

Not that I wanted to, but I felt that it would be more polite. But they all said at once that I was to stay and dine, and they wouldn't hear of me leaving.

In the end I went upstairs with Lady Marigold to wash my hands.

When we arrived in her bedroom she said:

"You have been a great success at my party, everyone asked who you were."

Of course I was thrilled and stammered something about how kind it was of her to ask me.

While she was powdering her nose she told her maid to pack up the dresses and have them sent back to the shop in the morning as she did not want them.

"Have a good time," she said to me, "and don't break my poor little brother's heart more cruelly than you can help."

Of course, I said I wasn't thinking of such a thing, but she answered:

"No, you may not be, but he is! And he is starvingly poor, so if you want a good dinner I should depend on Peter."

With that we went downstairs and there were the three men waiting for us. As we got into the hall Peter said:

"I have persuaded Lord Glaxly to let me look after you to-night."

Before I could say anything in reply, Pimples said:

"But will you dine with me to-morrow night instead?"

"Oh, thank you very much," I answered, "but are you quite certain that it is all right about to-night?"

Not that I wouldn't much rather have dined with Peter, but I didn't want Lady Marigold to be annoyed with me. Luckily she only laughed and said:

"You obviously brought your double-headed coin with you, Peter!"

The next thing I knew I was in the most magnificent Rolls-Royce with Peter and we were setting off to dine at the Aperitif Grill.

I was rather shy to start with, and then he was so amusing about everything and told me such lots of things I wanted to know about people and places that I began to enjoy myself enormously.

Everyone made a tremendous fuss of him at the Grill and he knew heaps of people there, and I couldn't help seeing that some of them were wondering who I was.

We had a most delicious dinner, and when we got back into the car he asked me where I lived, and when I told him he said:

"You will have to find somewhere better than that, it is hardly the right setting for you, is it?"

I said I had thought of it, but as I didn't know London very well yet, I thought I had better wait until I was more settled at Cantaloupe's.

"Nonsense," he said. "I will soon hear of something better for you and let you know!"

And as we got home he said:

"What are you doing this week-end? Come down and stay at my house in the country."

"I would love to," I answered. "Is there going to be a party?"

He gave me a quick glance when I said that and I have a sort of feeling that he hadn't thought of it until I asked, though I didn't ask from any reason except that I haven't got enough clothes for a smart party. But he said:

"Yes, I have asked one or two people, and I would like you to see the house."

Then he asked me to lunch with him to-morrow, and of course, I said I would love to. When we arrived he took my hand and kissed it, which was rather exciting, then I waved good-bye and the Rolls drove away.

It is funny, I like him very much, but I am rather frightened of him, he is so assured and sophisticated.

Now I should never feel frightened of Pimples, Lord or no Lord, he has not got the same manner, though his sister has a sort of easy superciliousness which is terrifying although I am sure she means to be kind.

I wonder what Peter said to Vera? And that reminds me, I forgot to ask Pimples what her other name is.

REFLECTION ELEVEN

Cleone has been an absolute brick and found me a little flat in the same building as herself.

When I say a flat, it is only one room with a tiny bathroom out of it, but she showed me how to make the bed look like a sofa in the daytime, and when I have got a few more things it will really look quite nice.

It is only 30s. a week because it is right at the top of the building, and there is no lift, but I like it as I can see right over the roofs and the sun comes pouring in in the morning.

It was rather awful leaving Bessie when it came to the point.

I was nearly in tears, mostly because I felt that I had been beastly to her even though it was her fault when she was so grumpy and disagreeable about all my new excitements. But she said:

"Good-bye, Linda, and don't get so grand that you forget all about me. I shall turn up one day like a bad penny and ask to have a peep at all the Dukes and Duchesses."

And I felt so bad about it all that I went out and bought her four pairs of silk stockings, and a pair of chiffon cami-knickers which I had seen in a shop in Shaftesbury

Avenue and which I knew was just what she would like.

She was terribly pleased, especially with the cami-knickers.

Of course, spending that money has made me a bit short this week, but I am economising enormously by going out to so many meals.

I talked to Cleone about moving and she asked whereabouts was I thinking of going.

I told her that Peter had said something about looking out for a flat for me, and she looked at me for a moment and then replied:

"Of course it is nothing to do with me, but do you think you are wise to make up your mind so quickly about him?"

"About him?" I answered.

And she said:

"Well, you don't suppose he is going to find you a flat unless he pays for it, and if he pays for it I suppose you will have to accept him in with the fixtures and fittings."

Of course I was absolutely horrified at that and said:

"I would never have thought of such a thing."

Cleone yawned and said:

"Well, I should if I were you, and if you take my advice, Linda, you won't let any man pay for the roof over your head, it is too uncomfortable if you have a row with them."

I answered quite hotly that I didn't intend anyone to pay for anything for me.

"Don't be a fool," Cleone said languidly. "I suppose you are going to buy yourself a fur coat and several new dresses out of four pounds a week!"

And that remark opened my eyes because I had wondered how all the girls at Cantaloupe's managed to have such marvellous clothes and expensive furs, if they had to buy them themselves.

Two days later Peter said:

"Oh, Linda, by the way, I expect you will want some extra things for a week-end in the country, I have sent Cantaloupe's a cheque for one hundred pounds for any little extras you will want. I expect you can get them at a discount."

"Oh, but I can't let you do that!" I exclaimed.

"It's only that," he answered, "you'll want special clothes you wouldn't have bought otherwise."

I was so bemused that I just said: "Thank you," before I remembered that I ought to have kept on refusing; but I must say it is the most thrilling thing that has happened to me in years.

I stammered a bit when I asked Madame Jean about it the next morning, but she took it as a matter of course and reduced all the things I wanted.

Now I have a wardrobe stocked with all sorts of marvellous clothes I feel quite confident about going down for the week-end—about my appearance at any rate—about the party itself I am not too sure, and about Peter I am not sure at all.

It was all rather queer last night. We have been out together four times since I met him.

Yesterday was the third evening, and when we were going back after dancing at some queer bottle club, Peter put his arm round me.

"We are going to be very happy together," he said, "aren't we, Linda?"

"You have made me awfully happy," I replied, "you have been so kind."

"May I come up and see your flat to-night?" he asked me.

I shook my head:

"It is not nearly ready for anyone to see yet, I want to get it all fixed up and nice first."

"A question of money?" he asked.

"Well, I can't afford to buy a lot of things straight off," I answered.

Then Peter took out his pocket-book and gave me five ten-pound notes.

"I can't take this, Peter," I protested. "It's absurd. You've given me all those lovely clothes for the week-end."

"What is money for except to spend on somebody beautiful like yourself, Linda?" he said lightly.

"No, I can't," I said, and put the money back into his pocket.

Then he tried to kiss me and I felt that if I let him kiss me he would expect me to take the money in payment.

So I twisted my head away and he only managed to kiss

the side of my cheek. He did not insist as I wa
he might, but just said:

"You are an exciting little devil, Linda!" and kiss
top of my shoulder as my cloak had fallen back.

Cleone's light was on as I went upstairs past her door
so I knocked, and when she called out "Come in," I found
her sitting in a dressing-gown in front of the electric fire.

Her flat is really lovely. She has two rooms, a bathroom
and a tiny kitchenette and it's all furnished in deep blue
with the walls painted to look like pine panelling. Awfully
rich-looking.

Then everything about Cleone appears very expensive
and she has some lovely jewellery!

"Had a good time?" she asked.

"Lovely," I answered. "And what do you think? Peter
wanted to give me fifty pounds to furnish my room."

Cleone raised her eyebrows.

"You don't do badly for an inexperienced one," she
said.

"I didn't take it," I said. "I thought it would be wrong."

"My dear baby!" Cleone exclaimed, "Peter is fair game
for everyone. He has broken more suburban hearts than
any other man in London . . . Are you in love with him?"

"Of course not!" I said. "Why, he is years older than
me."

Cleone looked at me with a strange expression in her
face—I can't describe it—kind and yet scornful.

"You are going down for the week-end to-morrow,
aren't you?" she asked.

I told her I was.

She was silent for a moment before she said slowly,
as if deliberating her words:

"Just what are you aiming at, Linda?"

I didn't quite understand what she meant and said so.

"That is what I thought," Cleone said, "I don't believe
you are aiming at anything. If that is true and if you take
my advice, you will play that innocent stuff for all you are
worth so long as you can, so lock your door to-morrow
night and don't argue about it if he questions you the
next morning."

"Do you mean to say . . . do you think that he will . . . ?"
I started to ask.

Then of course, I saw what a fool I had been. Of

61

course, Peter was only giving me presents and clothes because he thought I would become his mistress when he got me down to his house in the country.

"I shan't go!" I said.

"I should," Cleone answered, reaching for another cigarette.

"Why?" I asked.

"You will have to face up to the situation sooner or later whether you stay in London or go down to 'Whitefriars Park'."

"Shall I send back the clothes?" I asked, feeling suddenly miserable about the whole thing.

"Why should you?" Cleone answered. "Why should you, Linda? After all, if he likes to be a fool, that is his look out.

"Good Heavens," she added, "he has played the game often enough to know the rules. If you can only keep your head and not fall in love with him it will be the best lesson Master Peter has ever had."

"Why do you dislike him so much?" I said, struck by the very bitter note in her voice.

"Do you really want to know?" Cleone asked, almost savagely.

"If you don't mind telling me," I answered gently.

Cleone is usually so indifferent and languid about things that it was queer to see her roused.

She flicked her cigarette ash absent-mindedly into the electric fire and it left an untidy grey smudge on the blue carpet, but she took no notice.

"About ten years ago," she said, " a very pretty, very young and very silly girl came to London to 'seek her fortune' which she hoped would take the form of a rich husband. She came from poor but such respectable parents that they were considered 'country'.

"Her father was a retired Colonel and her mother struggled along on twopence a year to keep up a Lady Bountiful attitude towards the village which had belonged to the family for generations.

"Anyway, this girl had introductions to a large number of very nice people. She got a job in a shop and she had an exceedingly good time going out and enjoying herself one way and another.

"After she had been about for perhaps six months she

was on the verge of becoming engaged to a very suitable young man in the Foreign Office.

"He was not rich, but he certainly had prospects, and the girl liked him enormously, while he was crazily in love with her.

"It was just about that time that My Lord Rantoun came along. Attractive, sophisticated, with more money than he knew how to spend. He not only made violent love to the little country girl, but he loaded her with presents.

"Not money and clothes, she was too well brought up to think of accepting those, but books, flowers, sweets, scent and all the small things which society allows a young girl to accept from an admirer. She knew he was married, of course."

"Married!" I ejaculated. "Is Peter married?"

"Of course he is," said Cleone. "Didn't he tell you? His wife lives in Scotland—seldom comes South."

"I had no idea," I said weakly.

"Well, this other girl knew that, anyway," Cleone went on, "so she knew she was playing with fire when she went out with him and let him make love to her in his clever, practised way.

"Then she fell in love with him. Not in the sweet affectionate manner that she had loved the young man in the Foreign Office, but wildly, ecstatically, rapturously, which let her make a complete and absolute fool of herself.

"Peter was delighted, of course. It was, after all, what he wanted, and it was he who suggested that they should run away to Paris together, he who suggested that they should spend the spring on the Riviera waiting for his divorce.

"And the girl, poor silly little fool, agreed. She wrote to her young man in the Foreign Office, wrote to her relations, burned her boats and set off for Paris, ecstatically happy, absolutely certain that in a few months time she would be the Countess of Rantoun.

"Not that that position made the slightest difference to her, she was in such a maudlin state that she would have married Peter if his name had been Smith or Ramsbottom, the only thing she wanted was him and his love.

"It was a month before she found out the truth. A

month, I must own, of great happiness . . ."

Cleone paused, her cigarette had gone out.

"What?" I asked.

"Peter's wife will never divorce him whatever he does. She is a Roman Catholic, a very strict and orthodox one."

"But did Peter know that when he went away with you—with the girl?" I asked.

"Of course he knew it," Cleone said, "he had not even bothered to write to his wife as he had promised. He knew the situation and banked on it, as he had done before, time and time again. I was by no means the first."

Cleone dropped any pretence that she was telling me a story.

There was something in the wistful droop of her mouth, the sadness in her eyes as she finished speaking which made me get up and kneel down beside her chair.

"Cleone," I said, "you still love him?"

She looked at me blindly and then she got up and crushed out her cigarette in the ash-tray.

"Not really," she answered, "not now. I still hanker for the love I once had, but when I see him I hate him. And what is the use, anyway? He finished with me six months after our elopement—or rather, if I were honest, I should say four months. The last two he was bored, striving to escape."

"Poor Cleone! What happened to you afterwards?" I asked.

"Oh, I came back. My relations would have nothing more to do with me, of course, and most of my friends were too scandalised to know me.

"If Peter had married me, they would have been delighted to fawn on me, but as he didn't, it gave them a beautiful excuse to treat me like a scarlet woman, while they welcomed him back to the fold."

"And then you married," I said.

"And then I married," she answered and, getting up, walked to her dressing table to powder her nose.

She is very beautiful, even with her eyelashes un-made up. But I could see that she was tired, and there were unhappy lines round her eyes and round her mouth which showed that she was not as young as some of the other girls at Cantaloupe's.

I wanted to say more to her, to tell her how terribly

sorry I was, but I felt shy as well as bewildered by the tale she had told me.

While I hesitated the telephone bell rang and Cleone picked it up.

"Hello, darling, I hoped you would get away to telephone me," she said and with her free hand she blew me a kiss in dismissal.

I went out closing the door very quietly behind me, while Cleone was saying:

"You know I would love to do that, darling, it is always heaven when we are together!"

REFLECTION TWELVE

Whitefriars Park is really lovely.

It only took us about forty minutes to get from London and yet we might be miles away from any city. The gardens and the park extend for miles and the house is built on the top of a small hill and overlooks the whole country-side.

The house itself is Elizabethan, and I have never seen anything so beautiful as the red bricks which have gone a sort of deep rose-pink, I suppose with age and different sorts of weather.

Inside it is awfully comfortable with big family portraits round the walls and all kinds of treasures stored away in cabinets.

It fascinates me because I have never seen anything like it before, but the other people in the party take no notice, and when I said how lovely I thought a picture was of one of the first Earls of Rantoun, one of the girls giggled and said:

"Oh, Peter is not interested in Old Masters, are you? Only his new mistresses!" which I thought extremely bad taste.

It is extraordinary some of the things society people

say, even when they are terribly well-bred sometimes, one would have thought they would be too embarrassed.

It is an extraordinary mixed party too. There is a Cabinet Minister who spends his entire time trying to teach a little Mexican film star how to play golf. And there are two young men in the Brigade of Guards who play squash against each other and never seem to find time to talk to anybody.

There is an old man who everyone calls "Pop" and who seems to know more scandal and gossip than anyone in the world.

There is Lady Clare something or other, who is always racing and can talk of nothing else but horses. And another girl who is a great friend of hers, who is, as far as I can make out, busily engaged in trying to attract Peter's attention.

But Peter talks to me all the time and I sit on his right at meals, which seems queer, but everyone seems to take it as a matter of course.

Vera has been ringing up the whole week-end. I have found out that her name is Mrs. Croxton.

Her husband is a Member of Parliament and they don't get on and cannot have a divorce because it would affect him politically.

Anyhow I know she keeps ringing up because telephone messages are left in the hall on slips of paper, and I couldn't help seeing there were three for Peter all starting "Mrs. Croxton telephoned . . ."

Peter took no notice of them and put them into the fire, and that one gesture of his made me see even more clearly than Cleone's story how utterly ruthless he is when he has finished with a girl friend.

Last night when we arrived he didn't say anything which was in the slightest bit affectionate or that I could in any way construe into thinking was an amorous advance.

In fact, when he fetched me in the car, he was so friendly and ordinary that I began to think that he didn't care one hoot about me.

However, when he showed me my bedroom he took me into a big room overlooking the garden on the first floor and said:

"I hope you will be comfortable here, Linda, and if you want anything, my room is only just across the passage."

We changed for dinner, and when I got down Peter was shaking cocktails in a bar which he has had disguised as a bookcase.

It is very clever and when it is closed one would not imagine that there was anything so modern as a cocktail-shaker concealed behind the old leather-bound volumes.

He made me a cocktail and then he said quietly so that no one else could hear:

"You look absolutely marvellous, darling, but I am going to tell you all about that later on."

"This is where the trouble starts!" I thought to myself, so I opened my eyes wide and said:

"When?"

He went on shaking the silver shaker for a moment:

"Well, I shall have to tell you alone, shan't I?" he said, "and there are too many people here. Perhaps I had better come and say good-night."

He spoke lightly, but just too lightly to be natural.

"Oh, but Peter," I answered, "I am terribly tired to-night, I don't think that is an awfully good idea."

His face changed immediately.

"But, Linda . . . " he started to say, and then the little Mexican film star called across the room:

"A very strong cocktail for me, one with a 'kick' in it, please Peter!"

While he was answering her, I turned away and started a conversation with the Cabinet Minister, who tried to explain to me a bit of the trouble there seems to be about India.

I am afraid I didn't listen very much, but I must have looked as if I was, because after he had been talking for some time, he said:

"It is nice to find someone as young and beautiful as yourself, Miss Snell, interested in politics. You must come and have luncheon with me at the House one day, and I will show you round."

Luckily he sat next to me at dinner and I made him go on talking and talking much to the fury of the Mexican, and the amusement of the others who chaffed Peter about it.

After dinner we played some silly table games, which weren't much fun because the young men in the Brigade pretended to cheat and the girl who was trying to get off with Peter really did so, when no one was looking.

When it was eleven o'clock, I got up before anyone could stop me and said I was so tired that I must go to bed.

Instantly Peter jumped to his feet.

"I will see you upstairs," he said as he opened the door into the hall.

There was one of the footmen stoking up the fire so I quickly held out my hand.

"Good night, Peter, please don't bother, I can easily find my own way," I said, and slipped away before he could protest.

Upstairs I undressed, having first locked my bedroom door and the door from the bathroom into the passage, and then I jumped into the big four-poster bed and lay shivering and listening.

The fire-light was flickering on the ceiling and I could see the outlines of the lovely polished walnut furniture and the big vases of flowers which stood about the room.

Suddenly I thought how terribly funny it was. Here was I, Linda Snell, the illegitimate daughter of a trapeze artiste trembling with fright in case an Earl should get into her bedroom and make love to her!

I could not help giggling at the thought of it all.

It was funny that I should be sleeping in this enormous centuries-old bed instead of the property basket in a back street of some provincial lodging, and that hanging up in the cupboard were masses of Cantaloupe clothes!

Mine, all mine, who used to wear Ma's cut-down velveteens, or any old rags that no one else in the company wanted.

Laughing at myself made me forget to listen and so it gave me quite a jump when suddenly I heard the handle of the door rattle.

After a moment there came a little light knock, then Peter's voice saying:

"Linda!"

I lay quite still hardly daring to breathe; he knocked again, and still I took no notice.

Then I heard his footsteps going back across the passage and his bedroom door slammed.

I giggled last night, but here sitting up in bed with the most delicious breakfast in front of me and the sunshine pouring into the room and the maid drawing my bath next door, I cannot help feeling rather nervous in case Peter never speaks to me again.

It would be awful if he refused to let me stay the rest of the week-end. And after the way he treated Vera and Cleone, I am sure he is quite capable of telling me to go.

I know it is greedy, but I have eaten up every scrap of the breakfast and I've even finished a jug of cream on a perfectly luscious peach!

Well, whatever happens now, I shall be able to remember all these exciting things, and what is more I shall be able to keep all the clothes he has given me, so that I don't care if he is cross, anyway.

I shall just get up now, have my bath, put on my smartest new summer dress, and go down and face him.

REFLECTION THIRTEEN

It is funny that Bessie was right—and in spite of the fact that she herself never practised what she preached, her advice about men is certainly correct where Peter is concerned!

This morning when I woke up I lay for a few minutes looking at the blue walls in my tiny flat (I refuse to call it a bed-sitting room, it sounds so sordid).

Then I realized that someone was knocking and that was what had awakened me.

I jumped out of bed and put on a dressing-gown and opened the door and there was a messenger with a long flat parcel.

"Sign here, please!" he said.

When I looked at his book I saw it was not a district messenger, but one from Cartier.

Of course I could hardly wait until he had gone before I pulled back the curtains to let in the sunshine.

Then I opened my parcel, and inside was a perfectly lovely diamond bracelet. Packed with it was Peter's card and on it he had written:

"To make you think of me sometimes."

I have never seen such a lovely bracelet! And it is so

surprising, after the week-end, because I expected that by Sunday Peter would be seriously annoyed and have nothing more to do with me.

I have to send it back but I'm wearing it just while I get up.

I was really awfully nervous on Saturday, but there is no getting away from the fact that Peter's too clever to be obvious.

If he was annoyed about my locking the door, he never mentioned it, and was just the most charming and thoughtful host all through the day.

We swam in the swimming pool. There is a lovely one at Whitefriars, all blue tiles with comfortable coloured mattresses round it to lie on, and sun bathe.

We played tennis, and I was glad that I had practised so much at the Convent because, although Peter is very good, I was able to give him a game.

"What an amazing person you are, Linda," he said afterwards. "You look as though a puff of wind would blow you away and yet I believe that really you are stronger than most of us."

I think he was speaking the truth, because Lady Clare and her friend and the Mexican film star were dead-tired by the evening.

They just lay limply in chairs asking for cocktails to revive them, while I felt fine and went off and tried to play squash with one of the young officers.

I wasn't very good at that, and the ball kept springing off the back wall and hitting me. So we stopped and my partner said:

"What a little duffer you are!" and tried to kiss me.

When I told him not to, he said:

"No poaching on Peter's preserves, eh?"

That made me angry.

"It has nothing to do with Peter, or anyone else," I retorted. "As a matter of fact I haven't been kissed yet and I certainly don't want to start with you."

He looked at me quite incredulously for a moment.

"By George," he said, "I believe that is true—what an amazing thing!"

"Why amazing?" I asked. "Even a shop-girl has got to start sometime, you know; they are not just born messed about!"

At that he put his arm through mine.

"Look here, Linda," he said, "I am sorry, don't be cross with me. Just because I have grown used to finding things the other way, I wasn't expecting you to be . . . well, as you are."

We walked back to the house, and he was awfully kind and asked me to dine with him this week, which I shall do because I like him.

His name is Hugh Barlow, and now that we are friends he has stopped being sort of supercilious, and he talks to me and takes the trouble to see that I understand what the others are talking about.

That evening at dinner Lady Clare and her friend had some silly joke which they giggled and giggled over, and sniggered a bit too, rather like some of the girls at the Convent when they were talking about something *verboten*.

They tried to drag me into the conversation, but I didn't want to because I knew I should make a fool of myself, and Hugh said:

"Oh, stop it, Clare, you keep that sort of joke for the stable boys, they'd appreciate it more."

"Oh, but that is why we thought Miss Snell would like to hear it," Lady Clare answered, and turning to me added:

"It is true, isn't it, that your father was a groom?"

I knew then that she disliked me as much as her friend did, who was trying to get hold of Peter and was hourly getting more angry when he took no notice of her.

Everyone at the table waited for my reply, and just for a moment I thought frightfully quickly of what was the best thing to say.

Then I didn't see why these people should make me feel ashamed, so I said quite clearly and I hope defiantly:

"My father may have been a groom, to tell you the truth my mother is a little doubtful. But if it is of any interest to you, my stepfather keeps a pub, and quite a good one at that."

They all gave a sort of gasp for a moment, and then began talking as if they were embarrassed. Hugh squeezed my hand under the table—he was sitting on my left—

"Good for you, Linda," he whispered. "Clare is a little bitch."

I liked him for being on my side, but I didn't get a chance of speaking to him all the evening because Peter took me off to see some Eastern embroideries from China collected by his grandfather when he was Ambassador in Peking.

While we were looking at them he said:

"You are cruel to me, Linda."

And I knew that we were now going to talk about 'us', but I looked surprised.

"What a horrid thing to say," I answered. "I did hope that I had behaved well my first week-end in a country house."

"You know I don't mean that," he replied.

I shook my head and opened my eyes wide as if I didn't understand.

Quite suddenly he threw down the embroideries, caught hold of my hands, and when he spoke his voice was ardent and sort of eager, quite unlike his usual composed air.

"You are going to be nice to me, aren't you, Linda? Please, darling, I am crazy about you, absolutely crazy!"

"I haven't known you very long, you see," I answered in a soft, rather hesitating voice. "It is all rather frightening and I don't want to be rushed into things."

"I won't rush you, I promise you I won't rush you," he said. "But, Linda, let me come and talk to you to-night when the others are gone to bed. We are never alone with all this silly chattering crowd about."

I took my hand away from his.

"Oh, Peter," I said very reproachfully.

"I will be good," he said at once, "I promise I will—awfully good, and awfully kind, but let me."

"You are bullying me, Peter," I answered. "This is rushing me and I think it is horrid of you."

At that he became quite abject and kept saying:

"I will do anything to please you, Linda, anything. Only I do wish you would let me make you really happy."

"It won't make me happy," I said quite firmly, "if you try to rush me into things too quickly. After all I have only known you for a week."

After that, of course, I got my own way, though I took the precaution to lock my bedroom door again.

It is funny when I think over what I said . . . In a way it is true, even though I am acting it too. I don't honestly want to be rushed into anything.

I suppose really as Mummy's daughter I ought to jump

at the chance of living with Peter, and yet at the same time I feel deep down inside me that I might be one day in love properly—without thinking what I was getting out of it.

Money, diamond bracelets, even dinners and week-ends in a country house are all payments for love in a way. And I would like to be with a man for himself, and not because he was an Earl or a Lord or awfully rich.

It seems funny for me to be thinking like this when here am I sitting up in bed with Peter's present on my wrist. It looks simply lovely there, I must say, it sparkles in the sunshine when I move my arm.

Peter always gives me the impression he is playing a game. One is a pawn on his chessboard and I can imagine him saying:

"I will get a bracelet for Linda. That ought to dazzle the unsophisticated stepdaughter of a pub-keeper."

I am glad I told the truth to Lady Clare about who I was. At the same time I would love to know who my father was. Perhaps he would have felt at home at Whitefriars, or had a house just like it.

I wonder if Mummy had been clever he would have married her?

Once she told me that she was very, very much in love with him, and I imagine, like Cleone, she wouldn't say 'No'.

Anyway, I must now pack up the bracelet and send it back to Peter.

REFLECTION FOURTEEN

Oh, dear, things are really getting beyond me!

Peter is absolutely furious. Pimples is driving me mad with his eternal telephoning, and Hugh, who is really the nicest of them all, has chosen this moment to go into camp for manoevres or some other Army business.

Peter is really the problem.

I can cope with Pimples, though why he stands me being so rude to him I can't imagine; he is really rather pathetic, and sits for hours in his Club just in case I might want him.

Peter has been getting grumpier and grumpier and crosser and crosser. He has tried coaxing, pleading and bullying me, but now he is getting irritable.

The real truth of the matter is he is terrified that his friends at Black's Club will realise I am not living with him!

Just lately, as far as I can make out from Cleone and the other girls, someone has been spreading the rumour that Peter has not been so successful as he makes out, in fact that he is beginning to be chaffed about it.

Hugh and I were at the Embassy on Thursday evening, when the door opened and Peter came in.

Of course, I saw at once what he was up to because he

had Vera with him and she was looking like a tabby that has just finished off the cream.

She was beaming on everybody and fawning on Peter, who looked round the room until he saw me, then pretended he hadn't, and started to make a fuss of Vera, obviously for my benefit.

The whole plot was so obvious and Vera was making such a fool of herself, gazing into Peter's eyes and nestling her head against his shoulders as they danced by.

Men are bad actors and after the first half-hour or so Peter got bored and didn't play up. As Hugh and I got up to dance we passed their table, and I couldn't resist saying:

"Hello, Peter, how nice to see you here!"

He jumped to his feet, then introduced me to Vera who said:

"How do you do?" in the most frigid voice, looked down her nose at me, then gushed at Hugh for all she was worth. She was so rude that I thought I would just teach her a lesson.

"Aren't you going to dance with me, Peter?" I asked and smiled at him.

If Peter had been clever he would have refused, which would have been a score against me after the way I had behaved, but he didn't.

So we danced, leaving Hugh with Vera, who was so annoyed, Hugh told me afterwards, that she almost spluttered with rage.

Peter held me very tightly.

"This can't go on, Linda," he said.

"I quite agree with you," I answered, "the floor is much too crowded."

He gave me a little shake.

"Don't be so irritating. You know what I mean, you can't go on treating me like this."

"Why not?" I asked, waving over his shoulder to someone I knew.

"Because I won't stand it," he growled.

I shrugged my shoulders.

"Oh, well, darling," I answered, "that is up to you, of course!"

Then I made a few commonplace remarks about the

people and things in general before we got round to Vera's table. There I stopped.

"Do forgive me," I said to her, "for taking Peter away, but we are such old friends and had so much to talk about!"

And before she could think of a suitable repartee Hugh had sprung to his feet and we had moved away on the crowded dance floor.

We laughed about it, but I felt mean when I got home. So mean in fact that I sat down and wrote a little note to Peter, which was weak on my part, but somehow I hate being nasty to people, especially when they have been kind to me.

"Sorry, Peter," I wrote, *"I am a pig—Linda."* And sent it round by messenger to his house.

The next morning a box of roses arrived for me and a note asking me to lunch. When I got to the Ritz, Peter was waiting and I saw at once he was in a good humour.

When we had ordered, Peter said to me:

"Linda, I have got something to ask you."

"What is it?" I asked.

"Will you come away with me for good?" he said very seriously. "I will get my wife to divorce me and we will get marrried."

Just for a moment I couldn't believe my ears, and then I remembered that he did not know that Cleone had told me all about her *affaire* with him.

He must have seen her when he called at Cantaloupe's for me and he knew that she worked there, but there was no reason why he should imagine we had confided in each other, for I had never mentioned her to him.

It took me a moment or two to realise all this, and then I felt so disgusted with Peter for trying the same game with me as he had with Cleone over ten years ago, that instead of being clever and making some elusive reply I just said the first thing that came into my head.

"Good heavens, Peter," I said, "fancy trying that old trick on me!"

"What old trick?" he asked very sharply.

For the first time since I have known him he went quite pink in the face.

Then I realised that I mustn't give Cleone away. After all a rich man like Peter might do her some sort of harm, one never knows. If a man can get you into a job another man is just as likely to get you out of one. So I changed my voice.

"Do you know, you have never mentioned your wife to me before?"

"I know, Linda," he answered. "I can't talk about her, you must see that, but, of course, we don't get on and haven't for a great number of years.

"Perhaps she doesn't understand you," I said.

He looked at me quickly to see if I was laughing at him, but I kept my expression quite serious.

"Well, that sounds hackneyed," he muttered, "but it happens to be true, and she doesn't love me and I don't love her. Don't you think it would be a wonderful thing if you and I were really together, for ever and always, darling?"

"You are quite certain your wife would divorce you, Peter?" I asked.

"I am sure she would," he replied quickly, "if I gave her the right evidence. We will go away to Tahiti or somewhere really lovely until the talk and scandal has blown over. Say you will come, Linda. Please, my sweet?"

I dropped my eyes as though I was thinking very hard, then after a minute or two I asked:

"Why hasn't your wife divorced you before, Peter, if you haven't lived with her for so long?"

At that he hummed and hawed a bit and murmured something about scandal and washing one's dirty linen in public and a few other clichés we all know so well.

"I will think about it, Peter," I said quietly, "but perhaps it would be better if you could get a letter from your wife saying she will divorce you if you give her the evidence."

Luncheon after that was a rather a subdued meal, and when it was over we went back to Peter's house to try some new gramophone records which had just arrived for him from America.

I threw my coat and hat down on a chair and was just going to put one on when Peter gripped my shoulders and made me face him.

"You are playing with me, Linda," he said, giving me a sort of shake. "Are you playing with me?"

"You are hurting me, Peter," I cried, trying to escape,

but his hands were so strong I couldn't move.

"You don't care a damn, you want to hurt me, you are driving me mad! And I won't be tortured like this," he said.

With that he put his arms round me, tipped back my head and kissed me again and again so roughly that he hurt my mouth. It was quite useless to struggle although I tried.

Finally he let me go so suddenly that I stumbled against a sofa and had to hold on to it to stop myself from falling.

He was breathing very quickly and his eyes were dark, and blazing at me.

"There!" he said triumphantly. "I ought to have done that long ago, I have come to the end of my tether and you have either got to come away with me, or you can go to hell as far as I am concerned!"

I was too bewildered and surprised to say anything but just stare at him. Then I put my hand up to my mouth to see if it was bruised.

It was, and tears came into my eyes, more from shock than anything else. Peter saw them.

"Oh, hell," he said, "you had better go while I let you."

And with that he walked out of the room and slammed the door. After a minute or two I put on my hat and coat and let myself out into the street.

If that is being kissed, all I can say is that it's very disappointing.

I thought it would be much, much nicer!

REFLECTION FIFTEEN

Oh, I would give anything in the world to be able to telephone to Mummy and tell her what has happened.

But it wouldn't be very wise at this time of night; for one thing the telephone is in the bar and that will be closed, and secondly, she might be so excited that she would try to persuade me to accept.

But really when I think that I, Linda Snell, have just refused to marry a Lord, it does seem, as Bessie would put it, "a scream."

Of course, it's only old Pimples, and knowing him as well as I do now I am not as impressed as I might be, but still, a Lord is a Lord and there is no getting away from the fact that I should like to be "M'Lady".

A few moments after we had got into his car, Pimples produced a little box from his pocket, and inside was a perfectly lovely big square sapphire ring.

"Oh, Pimples, what a heavenly ring!" I exclaimed.

He stopped the car just where we were, against the kerb, and said:

"Linda, will you marry me?" rather breathlessly.

I was so surprised I couldn't think what to say, but just sat holding the ring in its little red box in my hands. I stared out of the windscreen trying to realise what was happening to me.

It sounds funny to say so, but I could think only of the traffic coming towards us, the lights of the cars and the swish-swish they made as they passed.

I simply could not imagine marrying Pimples. It did not seem a fact, it was sort of outside me, a queer question which was not true, like a kind of game of "What would you do if you were a millionaire?" or something like that.

As I didn't speak Pimples took one of my hands, started kissing it and saying over and over again:

"Do marry me, Linda, I do love you! Please marry me, Linda!"

And the awful thing was that he looked ludicrous. I suddenly felt that Lord or no Lord, I couldn't marry a man who was awkward.

"I don't know, Pimples," I said, "I wasn't expecting you to ask me this, it has surprised me!"

And immediately I said that, I laughed, because it sounded so like a startled Victorian Miss mouthing: "This is so sudden, Mr. Archibald!"

But Pimples didn't think it was funny. He pleaded with me. Then he was not only ludicrous, he was pathetic as well, and I hated the whole thing and felt I wanted to say:

"Oh, I don't know. Why do you worry me with questions like this?"

We stayed for hours in the road and Pimples did all the talking while I sat clutching the ring.

In the end because I was so sorry for him I said that I would wear the sapphire for a bit, on my right hand, of course, not on my engagement finger, and "think things over".

Pimples was terribly nice, but dreadfully humble and kept thanking me until I felt I would like to shake him and say:

"Don't be so servile, can't you see that I ought to be the one to thank you for offering to marry a little nobody like me."

But, of course, I didn't, and when I had gone into the flat he sat for simply ages outside, thinking of me, I suppose, because when I peeped out of my window a few minutes ago, he was only just moving off.

Now I am alone, I don't know what to think. My mind is in a complete whirl. I can hear Mummy saying:

"My, Linda! What a chance! And if you don't marry him you are crazy. Who are you waiting for, the Prince of Wales?"

REFLECTION SIXTEEN

Well, Peter is finished at last. We have just had a terrible row!

Of course it was due for some time, but I am sorry it has happened like this because I do hate being beastly to people who have been as kind to me as he has.

Not but when it comes down to brass tacks it has cost him much — the clothes for the country, lots of flowers, meals and several bottles of scent.

Cleone was partly to blame this morning, for she upset everyone at the shop by being over an hour late. Of course it would be a busy morning, we had two trousseau orders in.

Also, one of the girls had got into a row for borrowing a model coat without permission, and Cantaloupe had given her hell. So she was in a sulky temper too, which did not improve matters.

Anyhow, I was absolutely exhausted by luncheon time, my complexion had got mottled, my hair was a mess, and then a message came up to say that a gentleman was waiting for me.

I looked out of the window and saw Peter's Rolls so I knew who it was.

My first impulse was to say that I couldn't see him. It would have been wiser if I had, but I thought,

'Oh well, perhaps a good luncheon would make me feel better.'

So, I put on my dress, powdered my nose and hurried downstairs as quickly as I could, and just as I was ready Cleone said:

"You have a hole in your stocking," and there was a run right up the back of a new pair, and if there is anything more infuriating to a woman than that I would like to know what it is.

"I can't change now," I said, "but Peter will have to take me somewhere quiet. I can't go to the Ritz like this."

I told him so when I got downstairs.

"Oh, all right," he said, "we will go to the Maison Basque, although I had ordered your favorite table in the window at the Ritz."

That made me cross too. It is so irritating to know you can't do a thing because of something utterly trivial like a hole in your stocking, it is nearly as bad as having a spot on one's chin.

So when we arrived at the Maison Basque I was none too affable.

Peter might have guessed it was not the moment to start a scene, but of course, men are too abstruse for words.

As this was the first time we had met since the kissing episode, I suppose he was trying to get it off his chest; anyway, he started as soon as we had ordered.

"This can't go on," he said, and out came all the usual things he had said for weeks now without us getting any further.

"Oh, Peter," I said, "must we have all this over again? You know how it bores me."

"Does it?" he answered very bitterly and in a nasty tone of voice. "There is only one thing, as far as I know, that doesn't bore you, these days!

"What is that?" I asked, being curious.

He just shrugged his shoulders.

"I suppose it was absurd," he said, "my expecting you to be different from other women."

"I didn't know you were," I answered. "And, anyway, what exactly are you trying to say?"

At that he thumped the table quite angrily.

"I am trying to say that this one-sided business is not going on any longer. I have done everything I can for you—everything you will let me."

And at that I got really angry.

"If you think you can buy me you are much mistaken," I said, getting crosser every minute.

"I think you are extremely ungrateful," Peter said slowly.

That made me more angry than ever. Mostly because inside myself I think he is right.

"You should keep to people of your own age and your own class," I said. "I am sure they are more conversant with your methods than I am, and if you think that you can buy me for a few mouldy diamonds you are much mistaken.

"As for your offers of divorce, you can keep them to yourself. I would rather marry Pimples any day than have anything to do with you or your money!"

And with that I picked up my bag, leaving my food untouched on the plate and walked out.

I was in such a rage that I have walked straight up across Berkeley Square and into the Park, and I don't care if they are livid at the shop or what happens.

I have got to cool down before I can face anybody or anything, and I suppose I have been very silly, but occasionally one must be oneself and not always be acting and posing.

Of course I am all the angrier because I feel I am in the wrong although I am not half as ungrateful as Peter thinks.

REFLECTION SEVENTEEN

Bessie is in trouble and really ill.

Of course I would do anything in the world to help her, and it does seem rotten luck that it should have happened just now, because I am so hard up.

I've had to buy a lot of clothes to go to all the parties although Mr. Cantaloupe lets me have them very cheap. I've used up all my salary on them. Besides having to pay for a lot of my own meals, now Peter isn't there.

If only Bessie had come to me before, things would not have been so bad, but she got worried and went off to some filthy old woman round the corner who has very nearly killed her.

Of course I blame myself, because if I had been seeing her and that sort of thing she needn't have been like she is.

That cad Teddy went off and left her at once as soon as there was a hint of any trouble, and she has lain for the last three weeks in her lodgings having haemorrhage after haemorrhage.

If it hadn't been for her landlady, who, underneath a

very disagreeable manner, is kind-hearted, she would have been thrown out into the streets.

She didn't dare go to a hospital after what had happened, in case there was a scene about illegitimate practice and things.

So I don't know what would have happened if I hadn't gone up to see her yesterday evening.

I was feeling a bit low myself and just couldn't face Pimples or any of the other people I know. And I tossed up whether I should go and see Mummy or Bessie.

I didn't even know that Bessie was there, because a month ago she was talking about going on tour with some revue or other. Anyway, in the end I chanced it.

I thought a bit of cold common sense would do me good.

I rang the bell; the landlady came to the door and at once I sensed something was wrong.

"Is Bessie in?" I asked, and Mrs. Glaubel (that is the landlady's name) said:

"She is, and that is no thanks to her friends either!"

"What is the matter, Auntie?" I asked.

That was what we always used to call her because the only skivvy in the house was her niece, and we all got into the way of saying "Auntie" like she did.

Auntie folded her arms over her bodice and said:

"If you want my opinion she is dying!"

"Dying?" I echoed almost stupidly.

I thought for a moment she was playing a joke on me.

"If I wasn't a Christian woman," Auntie went on, "I should have turned her out long ago. I don't hold with things like that in my house, respectable I have always been, and Mr. Glaubel, he says to me:

'Gertie, you're a fool, that girl will get us into trouble, you mark my words, and if she dies there will be an enquiry, and then where shall we be I would like to know? Besides, there is five weeks' rent owing and no chance of us getting it either.'

After a few minutes I found out exactly what had happened, as far as Auntie knew it, of course, which was mostly from guess work because Bessie wasn't likely to have confided in her.

However, when I heard her version I tore up the stairs and there was Bessie in bed white as a sheet.

Her face had gone so thin I hardly recognised her, and her hair was lank and uncurled, with a great dark parting where the peroxide had grown out. She looked terrible.

The room was filthy, too, and I don't think the bed-clothes had been changed for weeks, but I couldn't say anything to Auntie after keeping Bessie there without the rent being paid.

I talked to Bessie and she told me what a fool she had been.

"And I knew of a better place," she said weakly, "only it was ten pounds, and I simply had not got it."

"Have you written to Teddy?" I asked.

She shook her head.

"I told him before it happened, and from that moment he has never come near me. It is no use blaming him, Linda," she added, seeing how angry I was, "he is a married man and it's my own fault; it's always the woman's fault."

"Oh, Bessie, why didn't you come to see me?" I said.

She gave a funny little smile, a sort of ghost of her old laugh.

"I felt the Dukes and Duchesses might not have a spare room, Linda," she answered.

And I could have cried at her joking when I knew all the time how terribly ill she was.

"I am going to get you out of this, Bessie, right away," I said.

"I can't go to a hospital," she answered quickly, and there was fear in her eyes.

"You will go to a private nursing-home," I said, "and I will get the best doctor in London to you."

"You can't afford it, Linda," she tried to argue.

"I am so rich, Bessie," I answered, "my second name is Rockefeller."

I went downstairs and told Auntie I would be back in an hour or so, and with the rent. I have never seen a woman cheer up so quickly.

"You have been a brick, Auntie," I said then, "I know that, but I wish you had let me know, I would have done something weeks ago."

With that I tumbled into a taxi and tore back here to find Cleone. She was marvellous, and when I had told her all about it, got on to her doctor who recommended a nursing-home and we fixed everything up. And she lent me £20.

The doctor came back with me and examined Bessie. He was awfully nice, not a bit up stage or grand, though, of course he knew exactly what was wrong.

He had an ambulance and a nurse sent for her, and they wrapped her up in a blanket and put her on a stretcher. She was a bit frightened of all this and hung on to my hand.

"You won't leave me, Linda, will you?" she kept saying, and I promised, but when I got to the nursing-home they would not let me into the operating-theatre.

I stayed downstairs, and I hope I never have to wait like that for a verdict again.

I walked up and down the room for what seemed to me hours and hours, until finally the doctor came in—the nice one—Cleone's friend, who had been with Bessie all the time although he didn't do the operation himself.

"I think it is all right, Miss Snell. Sir Arthur is very satisfied and we hope your friend will have a good night," he said.

When I had thanked him, I said:

"What is the fee going to be?"

He thought for a bit and then he answered:

"They will let you have a room here for fifteen pounds a week, you will have to pay that, but I know Sir Arthur will make a special reduction if I ask him. He usually charges one hundred and fifty guineas, but don't worry, he won't charge that this time.

"I am not grudging the money," I said quickly, "it is just a question of finding it."

"I know," he said, "but it won't be as much as that. I think about twenty-five guineas will be all right—he is a kind-hearted man I know. But if you had waited another twenty-four hours it would have been too late, so you will agree with me it was worth it."

I do think doctors are marvellous because I have often

heard how kind they are to poor girls, yet I had never realised it until now.

When I told Cleone she said that their charge in that nursing-home was twenty guineas a week, and that they were particularly kind and good to their patients, and that is why she was glad Bessie had gone there.

Doctor Edie—that is the nice doctor's name—says that Bessie will be there at least five or six weeks, so to-day I paid for two weeks right away and left the rest of the money for the operation fees.

"Oh, but you needn't pay yet," Dr. Edie said, but I preferred to give it while I could.

There are all sorts of extras I shall want money for, I can see that, because when I went round this morning to see Bessie the nurse said:

"Would you be kind enough to let us have some night-gowns for your friend, she is very short?"

They would not let me see her because she is not strong enough, but the nurse told me she had quite a good night and they hope I may be able to see her in a day or two.

At lunch time I went up to Tottenham Court Road to the lodgings.

Of course Auntie had not waited a moment before letting Bessie's room again and had jumbled up all her clothes and things into an old trunk in the attic. And I never thought things could have been in such a mess. I suppose my clothes in the old days must have been a bit like this.

Everything wanted cleaning and mending. And finally, I did find one night-gown which was not so bad, but all the others were completely unwearable. I do realise nowadays that cheap lace and bad chiffon doesn't pay in the long run.

While I was looking through Bessie's trunk I found Teddy's photograph and a couple of his letters she had kept.

There was not much in them, but somehow it made me mad that he should have gone away and left her like that— if he had sent her money I could have understood it better, but just to walk out on her was too much.

Of course Teddy was far too cute to put an address or any heading at the top of his letters, so I didn't know where I could get hold of him. I thought for a bit and then I decided that I could ring up Tony.

I should never have done it if it had been for myself. Tony had done me a jolly good turn and he wished to keep out of my life, but I was so mad for Bessie's sake that I went straight away and telephoned to his office.

When they said: "What name, please?" I said: "I am speaking for Mr. Cantaloupe," because I knew that would bring him to the telephone, and after a moment or two Tony's voice said:

"Hello!"

"Is that Tony?" I said.

"Who is it?" he said quickly.

"It's Linda," I answered, and I heard him give a little gasp, so went on, "I don't want to worry you, Tony, although I would like to thank you for all you have done for me. But I want to know Teddy's address—Edward, your friend—you know who I mean."

"Of course," he said, "but what do you want it for?"

"You had better know nothing about it, Tony," I answered, "and don't say you have given it to me or anything because I am going to give that man the fright of his life. You won't say anything, will you?"

He promised and gave me the telephone number. Then his voice changed:

"Are you all right, Linda?" he asked.

"Perfectly," I replied. "Are you happy, Tony?"

He hesitated for a moment and I felt I was being unkind, so I just said:

"Bless you, Tony, and the best of luck!" and put down the receiver before he spoke again.

I rang the number he had given me and the secretary answered me, and I asked what time Teddy would be in.

"Who is that speaking?" she asked.

"I am speaking for Mr. Robinson," I answered, choosing the first name that came into my head, "and it's a matter of urgent business."

"I will make an appointment for you for three o'clock," she said.

I thanked her and started off for the City.

I had taken the afternoon off from the shop anyway. I had told Madame Jean I had a photography job.

I got to the City just a few minutes before three o'clock and my heart was beating nineteen to the dozen when I was shown up to Teddy's office.

There were all sorts of clerks and people rushing about the passages, and they all stared at me rather curiously. The secretary was rather startled when I asked for my appointment.

"I thought you said Mr. Robinson," she said sharply.

"I did," I answered. "I have come here for Mr. Robinson."

"You can only have a few minutes," she said officiously. "We are very busy this afternoon."

"That will be quite all right," I replied.

A moment later a buzzer went on her desk; she opened another door and showed me in to Teddy's office.

Teddy was sitting at an enormous desk by a window with heaps of papers in front of him and a couple of telephones at his right hand.

The moment I saw him I realised what I had never done before, that he looked a cad and common, compared with Peter, Hugh or even Pimples. It was extraordinary how wrong he looked. I had always thought of him good-looking.

I don't know quite what it was, a sort of coarseness about his face, as well as the fact that his shirt was the wrong sort and that he wore a tie-pin stuck in his satin tie.

He looked up quite casually as I entered and then stared as if he had seen a ghost.

"Good heavens!" he said and started to his feet, "it is Linda?"

"Yes, it's Linda," I said with a smile. "How are you, Teddy, it's a long time since we met."

I swept across the room with my best society manner, shook him by the hand and sat down before he said anything.

"Is there anything I can do for you?" he asked rather nervously, moving the paper about on his desk, "I am afraid I can't give you much time, Linda, I am terribly busy to-day."

93

"Oh, I shan't take up much of your time," I said, "I just want a cheque for two hundred pounds."

"Two hundred pounds?" he spluttered. "What do you mean?"

"Exactly what I say," I answered, "and that is letting you off cheap, Teddy, so don't pretend it isn't."

"Now look here, Linda . . ." he started to say.

"You can stop all that!" I said sharply. "You have left Bessie in the lurch and she has very nearly died due to you—she is not out of danger yet."

"Well, I am sorry to hear that," Teddy said. "Of course it is none of my business and I can't hold myself in any way responsible."

"Whether you hold yourself responsible or not has got nothing to do with it—I hold you responsible, and you will either pay up or . . ."

"This is blackmail," Teddy interrupted. "I am not going to be blackmailed by you or any other cheap little harlot who comes round trying to pretend I have put her in the family way!"

"Yes, it is blackmail, Teddy, I mean it to be, too. What are you going to do about it, call a policeman and put me in charge?"

He was nonplussed for a moment.

"Well, don't bother to answer," I said, getting to my feet. "I see I can't prevail upon you to help. You wouldn't like to give me the address of your wife, would you, to save me the trouble of finding out? I have got a few letters I would like her to see, although I am sure my story will be sufficiently interesting in itself. Good-bye, Teddy!"

I walked towards the door.

"Blast you, this is blackmail!"

"I know, I admit it," I said grandly.

My hand was on the handle when he called: "Stop!"

"Look here, Linda," he said blusteringly. "I am not going to be bamboozled like this, but for old times' sake I will give you twenty-five pounds and we will call the whole thing quits."

"Two hundred pounds is the sum," I said, "I am not interested in anything less."

"I won't pay it," Teddy said, thrusting his hands into his pockets.

"All right," I said. "I don't care."

The door was actually open this time before he called out:

"Shut the blasted door and come back here."

I did as I was told.

"I will give you one hundred pounds," he said, "for the letters and an assurance that you will never come to me again."

"Two hundred pounds," I replied.

"One hundred and fifty," he parried.

"Just as it is you, Teddy, one hundred and ninety-nine pounds ten shillings."

I opened my bag and showed him the little bundle of letters.

He hesitated a moment and then cursing under his breath he got out his cheque book.

"If you stop the cheque I shall go straight to your wife and tell her my story, and somehow, Teddy, I think she will believe me."

"My god, Linda, I will get equal with you for this!"

"I should try," I said and laughed.

He handed me the cheque and absolutely snatched the letters from me.

"This will be a lesson to me," he snarled.

"I hope it will be," I replied, getting up, having put the cheque in my bag.

And then he looked at me and a nasty swimmy look came into his face.

"The least you could do is to give me a kiss for that," he said.

"It will cost you another hundred pounds if you come near me," I replied coldly.

"It is almost worth it," he answered, "you always were the one I wanted the moment I saw you. You would knock the spots off any girl I have ever seen."

I waited until he got quite close to me, still with that nasty look in his eyes, and then I gave him one of the hardest slaps in the face I could manage. It was vulgar, but I have never enjoyed anything so much.

"You can get out of my way," I said, "and keep out!"

And with that I flung open the door and went out leaving him swearing quite loudly.

The secretary gave me an awful look as I passed, but I ran downstairs and absolutely rushed to the bank.

It seemed to me ages before they finally passed the notes to me over the counter and I tucked them away safely in my bag; then I got into a bus almost singing out, I felt so triumphant.

I took the money and put £100 of it into my bank in Bessie's name. The rest I kept for the Nursing Home and the Doctor.

At least Teddy has had to pay up!

REFLECTION EIGHTEEN

Oh, God, don't let Bessie die...she mustn't die...
dear Bessie she loved life so...she enjoys everything so
much...it doesn't seem fair somehow that she should be
so ill...so bad that it's a question now of minutes...it
can't be true...they must have been saying that just to
frighten me!

Oh, God, don't let her die...let her live...I will do
anything...if only there was something I could do.

Last night when I went to bed I thought of Bessie as
getting well and spending the money I had managed to
get for her from Teddy. I was planning to tell her as soon
as she was well enough...she can't die...she mustn't.

How I despise myself when I think how little I have
done for Bessie after all she has done for me! If it hadn't
been for her where should I have been now? And what
have I done for her—not a damned thing...how I despise
myself...I could have given her so much pleasure...
and I didn't do it.

Oh, I know why I didn't do it...because I am a snob,
a horrible loathsome snob...I didn't want her to come to
the shop in case the girls should sneer at her—Bessie who
was worth the whole lot of them put together!

Why didn't I give Bessie a good time . . . if she lives I swear I will do everything in the world for her . . . I will give her everything I possess.

Why can't they come and tell me . . . another five minutes have gone by . . . it is no use bargaining with God . . .

If Bessie dies I shall never be happy again . . . I don't mean I shall always go about weeping and wailing . . . but I shall never forgive myself for leaving undone the things I ought to have done . . . funny that's a bit out of the Prayer Book . . . it's true, too, I have left undone all the things I might have done for Bessie.

I wonder if I ought to telephone the shop, I shall be late and I don't want to lose my job there, I am going to need every penny I can get for Bessie . . .

It is 9:30 . . . surely I shall hear soon . . . Bessie mustn't die—she is not to die . . . there is someone outside now . . . they are coming in . . . my heart is beating so fast I can't bear it . . . it is Dr. Edie . . . I can see his face . . .

Oh, God, I know what he is going to tell me!

REFLECTION NINETEEN

I suppose if one sat down and started to write one's life into a book it would either seem so dull that the reader would yawn, or say:

"Quite untrue to life!"

The last two days have been incredible, so incredible that I feel it is not me taking part in it at all but a stranger.

It is like watching oneself on the stage, yet at the same time it must be me, although my feelings are so chaotic, so overwhelming, that I shouldn't know how to begin to sort them out even if I wanted to.

I went to Bessie's funeral this morning, and even when I saw them shuffling the earth on to the coffin I felt it was all unreal and that it wasn't Bessie there at all.

If there is any sort of after-life I know that Bessie is happy, and that if she knows what is happening to me, she is also glad.

I paid for the funeral myself and I insisted on them giving her a coffin with silver handles. I know Bessie would have liked that, and it was the last thing I could do for her.

Harry took me to Kensal Green in his car, but he didn't come into the cemetery, he waited outside, and as I got back into the car again beside him, I suddenly thought it was appropriate that he should be there because it was all through Bessie we had met.

Perhaps it was meant that through her I should find the most wonderful thing in the world. She had given me so much it seems that even this had to come to me through her.

I wish she was alive. I would have loved to tell her all about Harry.

It is all so unusual and so strange, I keep going over and over in my mind what has happened since Dr. Edie told me Bessie was dead. He said something about blood-poisoning and some sort of fever.

I didn't cry, I don't think I said anything very much. He wanted me to have some brandy, but I wouldn't. I asked to see Bessie, but he said I had better wait until later in the afternoon.

I felt as if someone had given me a sharp blow on the head and I was just dazed and stupid.

All I remember after that, is finding myself walking in the Park saying over and over again:

"Bessie is dead! Bessie is dead! Bessie is dead!" in my footsteps.

I turned down by the Serpentine. It was a lovely day with bright sunshine and a tiny wind which made little waves on the water, and the seagulls were wheeling round some children who were feeding them with pieces of bread.

I walked on aimlessly, saying over and over again: "Bessie is dead." It didn't seem to make sense, they were just words, I couldn't feel that inside myself.

I stood still for a moment, looking across the water; the sunshine glittering on it, dazzled my eyes, and suddenly a big dog came past. It was an Alsatian and it came up to me in a friendly way.

Almost automatically, without thinking, I put out my hand to pat it, and it obviously thought I was going to play some sort of a game for it put a paw against my hand and gave a playful bark.

I don't know how it happened, but somehow a claw caught in a little bead bracelet I was wearing so that they broke and scattered all over the path.

Whether it was the shock I don't know, but as I bent down to pick them up I suddenly started to cry, the tears

100

streamed down my face and I couldn't stop them.

I was sobbing out loud when a very nice voice said: "I am sorry!"

But I just went on crying, and couldn't answer. Then I felt someone take my arm and lead me to a seat. I sat down, hiding my face, crying bitterly and hopelessly, for I suddenly realised that Bessie was dead. She had gone and I would never see her again!

After a long time I felt a big soft handkerchief put into my hand, and then I did make an effort to control myself, even though the sobs kept catching in my breath rather like hiccoughs.

Finally I managed to stammer: "I am . . . sorry!"

"It is all right, don't worry," the nice voice answered. "Jock didn't hurt you, did he? I have picked up your bracelet."

"It is not that," I faltered. "I wasn't crying because of that at all!"

Then I wiped my eyes and turned round to look at him. I found a big young man sitting beside me with a very brown face. He was hatless, and lying on the ground at my feet was Jock looking apologetic.

I blew my nose in his handkerchief.

"I am so sorry for behaving like this," I said, "but I have just been told that someone I loved very dearly is dead."

Of course when I said that the silly tears started again. I struggled to stop them.

"Cry," the young man said gently. "It doesn't matter and it's much better to cry and get it over."

"Does one get it over?" I asked weakly, catching my breath.

"Do you mean over death?" he asked. "Of course one does, death is very unimportant anyway."

"Is it?" I said, feeling too stupid to think, just asking questions feebly, yet happy somehow to have someone to talk to, someone to understand.

There was silence.

"Do you see what is opposite us?" he asked.

I looked and there was a little island in the middle of the Serpentine.

"That is Peter Pan's Island," he went on. "You remember what he said."

I shook my head.

"To die would be an awfully big adventure," he quoted.

"It is not much of an adventure for those who are left behind," I said bitterly.

"Don't you think that is rather selfish?" he asked.

That gave me an idea, perhaps it was selfish of me to want Bessie to live just so that I could make up to her for the things I hadn't done.

Somehow, I felt Bessie had not minded dying. If she knew anything about it, she would have met it as she met life—full of expectation and prepared to make the best of anything.

I thought for some time before I said:

"I think you are right, it will be an adventure to my friend."

"I often think about death," he said, "it's a subject which seems to present itself to me sometimes, and quite honestly what I feel myself is that if there is nothing when we die—just snuffing out like a candle—it doesn't matter much because we shan't know until it is too late.

"And if there is any continuity or survival, well, by the laws of evolution it ought to be a step forward, not a step backwards."

"I understand what you mean," I answered, "but you don't expect a nice golden heaven with a sapphire sea and a harp, do you?"

"Heaven forbid," he said fervently, and there was a hint of laughter in his voice.

I powdered my nose and I was horrified to see what a freak I looked. The young man watched me do it.

"Well now," he said, when I had finished, "don't you think we ought to start at the beginning?"

"The beginning of what?" I asked in surprise.

"The beginning of our acquaintanceship," he answered. "Now your nose is re-dressed I think we ought to be introduced."

I couldn't help smiling at him, he had such a funny way of saying things with a twinkle in his eyes. I handed him back his handkerchief.

"The only trouble," I said, "is who is to effect the introduction?"

"Jock seems to have done that very nicely for us already," he answered, "we must now exchange cards, but as I haven't got any, you will have to accept my credentials by word of mouth. My name is Harry Rumford, and yours?"

"Linda Snell," I said, and then added: "not *the* Harry Rumford?"

"It depends what you mean by '*the*'," he replied.

"The flyer," I answered. "Oh, but of course you are, I recognize you from your photographs. No wonder you are not concerned about death."

"Then it is *the* Mr. Rumford at your service," he said, bowing. "And I suppose you are *the* Miss Snell I have heard so much about?"

"What have you heard?" I asked suspiciously.

"That . . ." he started to say. "No, I don't think I will tell you, I expect you are much too spoiled already."

"Please tell me," I pleaded but he wouldn't.

After that I told him all about Bessie and somehow Harry is the sort of person one can't lie to—at least I can't, anyway—so I told him the truth, how mean I had been and how poorly I had repaid her kindness just because I was a snob, and he understood in the most marvellous way. All he said was:

"We all fail the people we are fond of, we all fall short of our own standards, if we ever completely achieved what we wanted for ourselves I think we should just die of conceit, don't you?"

Then he put out his hand and took mine.

"Poor little Linda," he said in such a nice voice. "I know just what you are feeling, but it is no use crying, that is the last thing Bessie would have wanted."

We walked back across the Park together to where he had left his car and he drove me to the shop, but only after I had promised that I would lunch with him at one-thirty.

Madame Jean was in a tearing temper when I arrived, ready to blow me sky high, but when she saw my face she calmed down and waited for an explanation, after which she was absolutely charming.

Cleone was nice, too, and helped me bathe my eyes. After an hour or so I began to look less of a freak.

I lunched with Harry in a tiny quiet little restaurant off Leicester Square, and then he took me to the nursing-home.

When we got there I suddenly felt panic-stricken.

"I can't go in, I can't," I whispered. "I have never seen anybody dead!"

"Don't Linda! Don't work yourself up," he said, holding my hand firmly, "there is nothing frightening, there to panic about, it's just Bessie. You are not frightened of her, are you? I will wait for you. Go up and see her. You will be happier afterwards that you have."

And, of course, he was right. When I walked into the room I wasn't a bit frightened, it was just Bessie lying on the bed.

A very white and thin Bessie, but she had a lovely smile on her face as if she had died quite happily. I had brought some flowers with me, lilies of the valley, I knew she would like them.

The Sister left me alone in the room. I felt I ought to kneel down and pray, but I didn't, I just stood looking at Bessie lying there with her eyes shut.

Suddenly I felt myself saying: "Bessie, Bessie!" just in case she was awake and could hear me. But of course, she did not answer.

I put out my hand and touched one of hers—it was very cold. I didn't know quite if I ought to kiss her or not, but I didn't want to.

She looked so peaceful and so away from everything I couldn't feel unhappy about her, it wasn't the real Bessie lying there, not the jolly laughing one I knew.

"Good-bye, Bessie," I said very quietly, in case she was hovering somewhere near and could hear me.

I told the Matron in the nursing-home that I wanted Bessie's funeral to be paid for by me and that the coffin was to be a very nice one; she quite understood and was very kind.

Outside into the sunshine I found Harry waiting for me and he never said a word, but just started the car and drove right out of London to Richmond Park.

We drove round and round for a long time until he stopped under a great clump of fir trees, where we were all alone, except for the deer.

Then Harry switched off the engine, turned towards me, put his arms round me and kissed me.

At that moment I knew that something very strange had

happened to me, something which had never happened to me before. I knew I loved Harry.

How long we sat there I don't know.

And love isn't a bit like I thought it would be, all sort of wildly exciting and queer, it's just absolute peace, and I never want to be anywhere else in the world except in Harry's arms, and to be close to him whatever he is doing or wherever we are.

We dined together that night and I can't remember anything we talked about, except that it was like a golden haze of happiness. When he drove me home he kissed me good night.

"I love you, Linda," he said gently, "and one day you and I are going to talk about lots of things, but now you are to go upstairs to bed and forget everything, except that you are happy and that we have found each other."

I thought I would never sleep with that strange mixture of happiness and unhappiness inside me and a sort of whirl of emotions which kept altering and changing in my mind, but strangely enough as soon as I got into bed I fell fast asleep.

I had such a queer dream that I remembered it next morning when I woke . . . I was in a dark tunnel, and I was looking for someone who had gone and whom I couldn't find.

I kept stumbling round with my hands in front of me, but I couldn't find my way, until suddenly I looked up and there looking down at me, as if they were on top of a wall, were Harry and Bessie.

"Come up, Linda," they said, and the sun was shining where they were so that their faces were all bright and shining too.

"How can I? Get me a ladder," I called.

"Oh, come on, Linda," they replied, laughing at me.

I tried to scramble up to them, but I awoke.

REFLECTION TWENTY

I love Harry.

It was all so perfect as I knew love would be if I met the right person, someone whom I loved and who loved me.

Harry loves me as much as I love him. The only thing that surprises me is that I should be allowed to know anything so wonderful as Harry's love. I don't want to remember that anyone else exists in the world.

There are a pile of telephone messages lying beside my bed now, but I don't want to see anyone but Harry ever again.

It is only five days to-day since I first met him and yet I can't remember what life was like without him, or how I ever imagined for a moment that I was enjoying myself with other people.

He is so strong and yet so kind, so possessive and yet at the same time, so tender.

We went out of London last night. Harry called for me about seven o'clock.

I just had time to get back from the shop to have a bath, and change into a soft green dress I have got, which looks like moss in Spring, when I heard the sound of his horn down below. I ran down-stairs.

"We are going for a picnic, Linda," he said. "Are you feeling countrified?"

One of Harry's pecularities is that he never says "Hello!" or "How do you do!" but he just starts a conversation as if we had been talking for sometime.

The sun had shrunk behind Windsor castle as we drove down the Great West Road and turned towards Maidenhead.

The sky was still yellow with just one evening star twinkling beside the ghost of the moon, and Harry murmured that it looked like an Arthur Rackham picture.

"Who is Arthur Rackham?" I asked, so he teased me and called me an "ignoramus."

"What can you expect from the daughter of an acrobat?" I said crossly, because I hated Harry thinking I was stupid.

"Agility," he laughed, and I had to laugh too.

Then he told me all sorts of beautiful things, and it surprises me how well read Harry is, and I can't think how he has ever had the time, because he has led a most eventful life, and one would not think he had a moment to spare for books.

We picnicked in the twilight on the river bank miles away from anywhere, and two white swans swam near us begging for the scraps.

After we had finished we lay on the rugs, talking and it got darker and darker until the moon rose and began to throw a silver light over everything, shimmering on the river until it looked enchanted.

After a time we grew silent and we didn't speak any more, and then suddenly Harry said:

"You know I am entering for this air race in a fortnight's time."

I had been dreaming, forgetting about everything but my love for Harry, and his voice made me jump, so that I sat up with a start.

"What air race?" I asked.

Of course I had not read the papers for days, what with being busy and everything, I never have time to see any of them, except the "Snob press" which is kept in the showroom.

But Harry didn't comment on my ignorance this time, he just said that the *Daily Racket* was offering £10,000 to the first aeroplane to reach Mongolia in the quickest time.

"A syndicate is backing me and I have promised to pilot their aeroplane," he added.

"It is safe, isn't it, Harry?" I asked. "There is no chance of your crashing or anything like that?"

"Oh, it is safe enough," he said, with a shrug of his shoulders, "but there is one thing which is worrying me, Linda."

"What is that?" I asked.

"I can't marry you until I come back," he said. "You see it is a question of life insurance. They have insured me in case anything happens to their aeroplane and I have got to give my word that I have no financial entanglements, so that there would be no possibility of a dispute about the money, just in case I mismanaged the machine or anything like that."

He was speaking lightly, but somehow I sensed that underneath he did not feel very frivolous about it all.

"There is danger?" I said. "You don't like the trip? Harry, tell me the truth, I want to know."

"Oh, there is no special danger, nothing unusual, Linda, it is not nearly so much of a strain as the transatlantic trip. Why, one can always come down if one is in trouble, and I promise you one thing, darling, I shan't take any needless risks now—it is only you I am worrying about . . ." He hesitated.

"Just in case?" I finished for him. "Harry darling,— I love you."

And when I said that he pulled me into his arms and held me very tightly to him.

"Do you mean that, Linda?" he said, his mouth against mine, "really mean it?"

I put my arms round his neck.

"I want you as my wife," he said.

"I will be your wife when you come back," I said, "but I will love you now."

"No," he answered, "I couldn't do anything that might hurt you in case I didn't . . . "

"Don't say it, "I interrupted. "I couldn't bear it if anything . . . happened to . . . you!"

"We've got to be sensible, my darling," Harry answered, "and I have no money to leave you."

I knew he was thinking I might have a baby, and I thought how wonderful it would be to bear Harry's child.

"What can we do?" I asked. "I must be with you. I must!"

"I'm not going to miss a second of us being together and being able to tell you how much I love you," Harry said. "But I won't make you really mine until we are married. I'm old fashioned, Linda."

"I am ... too," I answered. "There has ... never been ... anyone ..."

"Do you think you have to tell me that?" he asked.

Then he took me in his arms and said:

"You are so sweet, innocent and perfect, my darling. Just what I longed to find and thought couldn't exist!"

He kissed me until I couldn't breathe and I felt as if I melted into him.

Harry drove back to London with one hand and then he came up here into my flat.

How glad I am that it is so attractive, although I don't believe that it would have made any difference to either of us if it had been the barest and poorest of attics.

I undressed and he took me in his arms and kissed me, and kissed me.

But although I would have done anything he asked of me and sometimes we seemed to burn with a wild and wonderful fire, Harry never lost control of himself.

I wonder how any one can ever laugh or makes jokes about love, it is such a beautiful thing, almost sacred and I don't know how women can bear to have the memory of it sneered at by red-nosed comedians or laughed at by cocktail-drinking fools.

I only know that loving Harry is so perfect that I would kill anybody who laughed about us.

It was dawn when he left me and before he went he drew back the curtains so that we could see the sun shining very faintly on the chimney pots.

Harry looked out and then he drew the curtains back again, came over to me and kissed me very, very gently.

"Good-night, my little love, go to sleep again, I will telephone you in the morning."

I put out my hands and tried to hold him, but in a moment he was gone and the door shut very gently behind him.

I could still smell the faint scent of his hair on my pillow as I snuggled down under the bed clothes.

Now I am awake again and it is nearly nine o'clock. In one minute I shall have to get up and simply rush to the shop.

It all seems so beautiful and so incredible that perhaps I have dreamt it. But when I think of Harry I feel little thrills of excitement running all over me, and I know no dream could make me so excited, and so he must be real —is real—my own husband to be!

REFLECTION TWENTY-ONE

I didn't know that any sea could be so blue. Devonshire is exactly what I imagined the Mediterranean would be like.

Lying here on the sands the sea is the colour of the Madonna's robe in the convent chapel, and the rocks of the little island at the mouth of the river are deep red.

This is the most lovely place I have ever seen and only Harry could know of anywhere so beautiful and so peaceful.

We call this our 'pretend honeymoon' and the funny old Devonshire couple who keep the little inn where we are staying think we are just married, and are perfectly sweet to us.

No ceremony performed by parson or angel could make us happier than we are.

From our windows we can see the sea and there are texts on the wall worked in wool and beads, and the only light we have at night are two candles in heavy brass candlesticks.

It is all so very simple, very clean, and the food is delicious, fresh fish and lobsters brought in by the fishermen every morning, and home-cured hams, and pork pies which the old lady makes herself.

Harry drinks draught beer out of great pewter mugs and I drink cider, which I find far more intoxicating than any champagne or cocktails.

We are awfully happy and if we could live like this when we are married I should never ask for anything better.

Most of the day we lie, as I am now doing, on the beach, cooling ourselves in the water when the sun gets too hot.

Goodness knows what my skin will look like when I get back to the shop, but I don't care and they must just put up with it.

Cantaloupe was inclined to be very snorty when I asked for a week's holiday, but Madame Jean told him about Bessie, and after that he was quite sympathetic and agreed that I could go.

Although owing to the short time I had been at the shop, I would not be entitled to any money for the time I was away.

I felt rather mean using Bessie as an excuse except that she would not have minded, she would have been delighted if she could help me to happiness.

I don't quite know what we will do when we are married, because all we will have to start with is £5000, that is if Harry wins the race.

He gets half the prize money and the other half goes to his backers. I never thought much about it, but if I had I should have imagined he had lots of money.

He wears the most expensive looking clothes from the very best tailor, and his car is the very latest type, but it is only lent to him as an advertisement.

And, as a matter of fact, he has no income at all except what he earns flying, which, of course, is very little as he can't do records every day of the week.

In between special trips and races he has the greatest difficulty to keep himself going. He gets a bit from advertising special oils and different machines, but on the whole I quite see he can hardly keep himself, let alone me.

Not that I wouldn't work my fingers to the bone for Harry, and I don't mind how poor we are as long as we are together. But it is worrying.

There was not even enough money for us to come down here, if I hadn't pawned Pimple's ring. Goodness knows

112

what I shall say to Pimples because I must give him his ring back and tell him once and for all it is no use hanging about waiting to marry me.

But I will manage these problems somehow when Harry has gone, I don't want to worry him about them. I told him the sapphire was mine, and we got £70 on that and another £15 on Harry's watch and gold links.

Of course we have spent nothing like that at the Sloop Inn. It is awfully cheap and so is the food, but we both wanted to be on the safe side, and, of course, the car simply eats petrol.

It is funny that Harry should be as poor as I am. His father was a schoolmaster in Wales, he pinched and saved to send his son to a public school, and then Harry's last term he died leaving absolutely nothing as he had commuted all his savings into an annuity.

So at eighteen, Harry was left without a penny, and without any assets other than a public school education, which he says fits you for nothing except a leisured existence.

Somehow or other, he managed to get into some motor works, took up racing at Brooklands, did awfully well, and managed to meet influential people.

They finally took an interest in him when he started flying and gave him a chance of competing in the first race from London to Capetown, which he won.

Harry is twenty-eight now, and I suppose he is one of the most famous pilots in the world, so it does seem to me absurd that a grateful country can't vote him just a little money, at least enough to save him worrying where his next meal is coming from.

As a matter of fact Harry never worries himself, he is always saying that everything is for the best and that something will turn up.

I wish this beastly race wasn't getting nearer and nearer. Harry is determined to win it because of me. But yesterday I said:

"No money, Harry, is worth your taking the slightest risk. You do see that, don't you, darling? After all, we would rather die of starvation together than for one of us to be left alone."

"Shut up, Linda," he replied at once, "don't be a little silly!"

But I couldn't help being silly and a big sob came before I could stop it as I said:

" . . . and that . . . one will be . . . me!"

Of course, after that Harry kissed me and said that I was a goose to worry, that aeroplanes these days are as safe as buses, and that if I went on frightening him, he would lose his nerve, refuse to go at all.

Then no one would say he was "*the*" Mr. Rumford, and I would be so disappointed because I wouldn't be able to be "*the*" Mrs. Rumford.

I see Harry now, swimming in the sea, and in a minute he will come running back towards me over the sands. He will throw himself down beside me or bend down and kiss me so that the salt water drips off him on me.

He is so handsome, so divine. Oh! He is not coming in, he is swimming out again. I will go down and join him.

I am jealous even of the sea if it keeps him away from me for too long.

REFLECTION TWENTY-TWO

A rather tiresome thing has just happened. Pimples has arrived at the Sloop Inn.

We were coming back from the beach for lunch when, as we walked up the street, which is a pretentious name for a mere track leading to two or three thatched cottages, I saw standing outside the hotel a big yellow car.

"I say, that's a nuisance," I said to Harry. "There are some people arrived, I hope they are not going to stay."

"Oh, hell!" Harry answered.

Then as I got nearer I thought I recognised the car, and suddenly I guessed.

"It's Pimples," I exclaimed, and we both stopped dead.

I had written to Pimples when I was going away from London, thinking that he would bombard the shop, and the flat if I just left without leaving an address.

So I wrote him saying that I was so upset by my friend's death that I was going to Devonshire for a few days by myself to be quiet, and that I would ring him up immediately I returned.

The last thing I expected was that he would come rushing after me, although, of course, it was terribly silly of me to have put where I was going—but one would have thought Devonshire was vague enough.

It seems difficult when I compare him with Harry to believe that Pimples loves me too, and I suppose really one ought to take it as a compliment.

Now it makes me so impatient even though I admit that before I met Harry I was rather pleased when men made a fuss of me.

But I can't bear the idea of seeing anyone else at the moment. It's absolute agony to think this idiot Pimples may spoil even an hour of our perfect time together.

"I will go and tell him to go to the devil," I said angrily.

But Harry seized me by the arm and took me down a little side path which led to the back door of the inn.

"Why not let me send him away?" I asked wonderingly.

But Harry just said: "Shush!" and we crept in by the back way and up the stairs.

I could hear Pimples' voice in the bar, because the house is tiny and he was talking rather loudly to the old inn-keeper. I wanted to listen to what he was saying, but Harry hurried me into our bedroom.

"Now explain," I said, when he had shut the door.

He thrust his hands deep into the pockets of his grey flannel trousers, and stared at me rather grimly.

"Let's get married," he said.

"But you can't, Harry," I answered, "you said so."

"We could do it secretly," he said, kicking the foot of the bed with his foot, "or else I can chuck the whole thing."

"Don't be so silly," I answered, "as if *you* could get married secretly; why, the very moment you put your name down at the Register Office the news would be telephoned to London and it would be in all the evening papers. But why all this? Surely you are not jealous of Pimples?"

Harry sat down on the bed beside me and put his arm round my waist.

"I am not jealous, my sweet," he said, "but don't you know that if that fellow finds you and me together here, it's going to make it so much more difficult for you?"

"Difficult for me?" I echoed. "Why?"

"I see things like this," Harry said seriously. "You have told me a bit about your life, and I think that while you have had amazing luck, you have, to put it bluntly, got away with a good deal. Now, Linda, let us face facts. The reason you have been able to manage Rantoun and those others is simply because you are innocent.

"Don't interrupt—I know what I am talking about. Any man who has got any form of decency in him respects a girl when she is a virgin.

"But if when you go back to London they think you have had a lover, there is absolutely no excuse for you not to take dozens more.

"You don't suppose that Rantoun and Glaxly won't make things pretty uncomfortable for you because they think I have succeeded where they have failed?

"Of course they will, darling, it is only human nature, and I don't want to put you in that position while I am away."

"But, Harry," I said, "you will only be gone a fortnight. You don't suppose I am going to be out every night enjoying myself and gadding about while you are risking your life, do you?"

"I don't know? I don't know what to think," Harry answered, getting up and walking round the tiny room, "but I feel that we ought to keep our 'pretend honeymoon'.

"It is not because I am ashamed of it," he added seeing my face. "Don't be a little silly, I adore and worship you, I would like to put it in headlines in the papers and shout it through the wireless and paste it on all the hoardings 'Linda Snell belongs to me'. You know as well as I do no one would believe I am not your lover and instinct tells me that it might make things more difficult for you."

"I understand, Harry," I said, "of course I understand, and I am sure you are right.

He took my chin in his hand, tipped my head back and kissed me, a long lingering kiss.

After which he picked up a pillow and threw it at me, and we had a mad absurd game with it, which ended in us both getting very hot and very ruffled and in my having to remake the bed, we had got it into such a mess.

"Heavens! I am hungry," I said, when we had calmed down again. "It's nearly two o'clock, do go downstairs and get some food."

"All right," said Harry, "I shall say you are lying down with a headache—a touch of the sun—but, nevertheless, you have got a healthy appetite."

"That is true enough," I said.

"I will try to avoid seeing Glaxly," he went on, "but it really doesn't matter because we are registered as Mr. and Mrs. Robinson, and if he does know me he is in honour bound not to tell as one gentleman to another."

In about five minutes he reappeared with, thank goodness, a huge slice of pork pie and a bowl of raspberries and Devonshire cream.

"Did he see you?" I asked.

"Unfortunately, yes," Harry replied. "I wanted to kick the little swine down the steps. He said:

" 'Hello, Rumford, fancy seeing you here!'

"I realised my best course was to be affable, so I asked him not to call me by my real name and not to tell anyone where I was.

" 'I am resting before the race,' I said very solemnly, and of course after that he could only promise to preserve my secret and wish me luck on the fourteenth.

"Then of course, just as I had settled things nicely the old woman comes waddling along saying how grieved she was to hear that you had a headache and would you like her to send over to Kingsriver for the local doctor.

"I assured her that there was no cause for alarm, but of course, Glaxly was listening. He dug me in the ribs with a leer:

" 'Didn't know you were married,' he chortled, and again I had the greatest temptation not to give him a swift kick in the pants.

"However, I dug him back a great deal more strongly than he expected and said:

" 'Mum's the word.' Then we went on talking about aeroplanes."

"Oh, Harry, I do wish I had seen you," I giggled. "Has he gone?"

"That is the bore," Harry said, helping himself to some of the raspberries, "he has settled himself down with a glass of port and a cigar and looks as though he will be here for hours, so we shall just have to stay in until he chooses to move. He has been making enquiries about you too, in the bar, but of course nobody has heard of Miss Snell, and so perhaps he will soon take his sleuthy ways elsewhere."

"Pimples as Sherlock Holmes," I laughed. "You must

say it is funny, but do you think it is just chance that brought him here?"

"I think so," Harry answered. "I don't think we need worry, and anyway unless he sees you, Mrs. Robinson is a pretty good blind."

And so here I am stuck in the whole afternoon while Harry keeps going downstairs to see if Pimples has moved.

He has just gone down again for the fifth time, bless him.

It is funny when you love someone there doesn't seem to be a minute when you are not bursting to be with them because there are such heaps of things you want to say. Oh, I hear him coming back!

REFLECTION TWENTY-THREE

I could hardly bear to face the girls this morning when I got back to the shop. They greeted me with cries of: "How sunburnt you are, Linda!" "Where did you go?" "Do tell us where you have been!"

They were all very pleasant, but at the same time I could see they were dying with curiosity to know what I had been up to. Even Madame Jean said:

"Your holiday seems to have suited you, Linda, but I don't know what Mr. Cantaloupe will say about your sunburn. He wants to design a new model on you this morning, so you will soon find out what he thinks!"

When I got a moment alone with Cleone I asked her if she had anything to tell me. She was the only person who knew where I had gone and with whom, and of course, I knew I could trust her with any secret.

"Pimples drove me nearly mad," she said. "He rang up the flat every day to find out if I had heard from you, and I knew he went down to Devonshire for the week-end to see if he could find you."

"I know," I answered, "he turned up where we were staying, but I hid so he didn't find me."

I told her what Harry had said about keeping everything secret while he was away.

"He is quite right," Cleone said. "I wondered myself how you were going to face the others, but if you can keep it from them you will be all right."

"Really!" I said, half-laughing and half-serious. "You and Harry seem to have got it into your heads that people are waiting round every corner to pounce on me. I am beginning to get quite nervous!"

"You have certainly got Pimples into a nice state," Cleone answered.

And then, before we could discuss matters any further, a message came up that Mr. Cantaloupe was waiting for me.

He was in one of his bad tempers. He always gets into one when he is designing—artistic temperament, I suppose! —and when I entered his room there was a row going on about materials.

"This is not the design I ordered!" he was storming, undoing yards of the most gorgeous brocades, which looked to me quite lovely enough as they were.

He ignored me for some time, and then finally he said sharply, as if he had been waiting for me:

"Come along, Linda, let me get this pinned on to you."

I slipped off my kimono and stepped on to the model throne in the tight satin slip which is all we wear for designing. He took up several yards of oyster satin and threw them over my shoulder, and then for the first time noticed my sunburn.

"What have you been doing?" he said, looking at my arms and my neck. "My dear child, it is positively Hawaiian!"

He stood back staring at me.

I thought for a moment he was going to be really angry, but he changed his mind, secretly I think it was because the sunburn does suit me.

Harry tells me I look a hundred times lovelier brown than lily-white.

Anyway, apart from that I am not such a fool as I was about my looks, and with my very fair hair I can see that sunburn is rather striking, especially as I have gone a pale coffee-colour, not a bit red or rusty like some of the girls.

"Bring me the dead white georgette," Mr. Cantaloupe said to Madame Jean.

In about ten minutes he had created the most lovely dress on me I have ever seen—absolutely plain, with just a touch of silver at the waist and at the hem!

It really is quite perfect with a brown skin, and I would give anything to have it for myself, but I don't think that is likely!

This afternoon seemed interminable. It seems impossible that only yesterday morning I was lying on the beach with nothing to do and nobody to order me about except my beloved Harry.

We were so happy, although returning to London was like coming back to prison.

I feel rather guilty about our bankrupt state, because we had twenty-five pounds left when we left Devonshire, but as we came through Bristol Harry said:

"I am going to get you something to wear, Linda. It is no use saying don't be extravagant, because I am just going to be. So stop here and don't dare move until I come back."

Then he parked the car and me outside a jeweller's and disappeared for ages! He came back with the most divine ring all encrusted with tiny diamonds, and he put it on my finger and kissed it.

Of course I was absolutely thrilled and simply adored my present so that I hadn't got the heart to scold him, when he told me he was left with only four pounds and that we should want that these last two days together!

I have ordered a present for him too, since I have come back to London, though goodness knows when I shall be able to pay for it.

It's a tiny gold aeroplane, and I am going to put it on his watch-chain when he takes me out to dinner to-night and I know he will be pleased because underneath it is written:

"With all my love—Linda."

Although it sounds conceited I know that Harry would rather have my love than all the money in the world.

I shan't be able to see Harry until awfully late to-night because he will be down at the aerodrome all day and on Wednesday morning he leaves at dawn!

Seven-thirty, I think, the zero hour is. Then I shall have

to come back here just as though nothing has happened and I suppose I shall bear it, but I don't know quite how.

Whatever happens I mustn't upset him before he goes. I must pretend that I am perfectly happy and quite confident about it all.

I try to think myself into being brave but I know I am just dreading Wednesday with the most miserable cowardice!

But whatever happens I mustn't let Harry know because it might upset him and then he won't win the Race.

REFLECTION TWENTY-FOUR

God bring him back safely, my Harry . . .

There he goes! . . . His aeroplane's circling round now
. . . I don't suppose he can hear everyone cheering . . .
there is the Prince of Wales over there, he said: "Good
luck, Harry!"

I wish these damned tears didn't make everything misty,
I can't see . . . There he goes now, getting quite faint in
the distance. . .

"Good-bye, my Harry, take care of yourself . . . I will
pray for you every moment, every second . . . Good-bye,
my darling, even though you can't hear me."

Fancy all these people getting up so early in the morning. They love Harry, but not as much as I do, but they
love him, they are cheering him.

They cheered him when he arrived and they all rushed
round him. A woman put a piece of white heather into
his hand and he put it into his button-hole.

But it isn't that that is going to bring him luck, it is
my little gold aeroplane. He has got it in his pocket, next
to his heart, he said, and he had got a snapshot of me,
too—such a funny one.

Not the pretty one I would have liked him to have

chosen, but one of me on the beach in my bathing-dress, laughing because the sun was in my eyes.

I wanted him to have one of me where I looked lovely against some green trees, but he wouldn't.

"This is my Linda," he said, picking up the one of me on the beach, "that is how you look for me, darling, the others are posed—the Society Linda that I don't like."

I wish I could have gone with him in his pocket instead of my photograph. I can't see his aeroplane any more, it is out of sight. One of the others is starting off—what a noise—and everyone is cheering all over again and waving.

When we got here everything was in too much of a whirl for me to think coherently.

Everybody was talking at once and wishing him luck and giving him last instructions and goodness knows what else.

I walked about alone for a bit, and then someone shouted: "Rumford's off!" and his aeroplane was taxied on to the field.

I thought for one awful moment he was going without saying good-bye to me, and then he came on to the field with the Prince and all sorts of other people.

He came straight across to me and kissed me in front of them all.

"Goodbye, my own Linda," he whispered against my ear. "Don't worry, darling."

"Take care of yourself, sweetheart," I said, and then he was gone.

I expect they will put all sorts of pictures in the papers to-night of me saying good-bye to him, but I don't care!

We will be married in a fortnight from now anyway, and then people will have to connect our names together whether they like it or not.

Oh, here is the car.

Thank goodness I haven't got to talk to anyone on the way home, I can think about Harry, and if I do cry no one will know.

REFLECTION TWENTY-FIVE

Harry is leading! The posters have got *"Harry ahead"* on them. I can hardly believe it, I am so excited.

The German 'plane is second and then the Dutch, and the other two English aeroplanes who have entered are miles behind.

Oh, I am proud of Harry, so proud of him! The most difficult thing in the world is to stop people from knowing how much he means to me, because everyone is talking about him and about the Race.

Whenever I see his name on the posters it just makes my heart leap with excitement.

Oh, he must be so pleased himself. And it is all due to my own mascot, and perhaps a bit to the "laughing Linda" in his pocket.

I wonder if he is thinking of me as much as I am thinking of him?

I went to bed last night and couldn't sleep for ages. The papers said that yesterday's visibility had been bad and that some of the aeroplanes had got into bad thunderstorms.

They did not mention Harry except to say that he was all right. This morning I got up frightfully early so as to go out and buy the morning papers, and the first thing I saw as I came into the street was the poster with Harry's name on it.

The *Daily Express* had him in headlines and pictures of him kissing me good-bye, but it didn't say my name, only:

"Harry Rumford, England's hope in the London—Mongolia Race, bids farewell to a friend."

I didn't say a word when I got back to the shop and only Cleone knew how difficult it was for me to be natural. I thought the morning would never end.

As soon as I could get out for luncheon I rushed to the Berkeley to look at the tape-machine.

The evening papers told us very little and I spent most of the evening at the Berkeley again, but there wasn't much news, only just a brief reference to Harry as he passed over different towns.

It is nearly one o'clock, in another five minutes I shall be able to rush to the Berkeley. I'm letting Pimples give me lunch so that I can look at the tape.

I suppose Pimples will ask me to marry him again, he does that regularly.

I hope I don't get so excited about Harry that I encourage him. I mustn't do that whatever happens, Pimples doesn't need encouragement.

Only three more minutes—I think I see Pimples' car outside. Oh, joy, just a few minutes and I shall know how my Harry is!

REFLECTION TWENTY-SIX

I wish I hadn't come out to-night. I would much rather have stayed at home. Pimples persuaded me and here we are mixed up with one of Lady Marigold's noisy parties.

I wonder why I ever thought the Savoy was the most exciting place in the world? I think to-night it is awful. I hate the people, and I hate the band. And most of all I hate the people who are with us.

If it wasn't so rude to Lady Marigold I would have gone home long ago, but she has always been very kind and I hate to be impolite, especially as I know Pimples insisted on us joining her party whether she wanted us or not.

Pimples is sulking at the moment because I was rude to him, and so he has gone off to dance with a shrill-voiced American girl who is making a great fuss of him.

I was disagreeable because I couldn't think what else to say when he asked me why I wasn't wearing his sapphire ring, so I said:

"I didn't want to to-night."

"I do think you might wear my presents instead of that cheap diamond thing you have got on your hand," he said sulkily.

Of course, referring to Harry's ring in that way made me wild.

"Leave me alone," I answered, "can't I wear what I like without having to ask you? If you go on like this I shall refuse to see you and that will serve you right."

Full of affronted dignity Pimples has gone away and now I am left with one of the half-baked young men. I wonder if I could slip away and have a look at the tape machine.

I could pretend I wanted to powder my nose—that is a good idea . . .

I managed that quite well. I thought the idiot would insist on coming with me, in which case I should have had to go into the cloakroom. I wonder where the machine is? I will ask this man . . .

It is not true what he says! It can't be true! He doesn't know what he is talking about! Where is the tape? Yes, it is there. It is written:

Harry Rumford in Speedway 660 crashed over Mount Lenix, 'plane down in flames, pilot reported dead.

It can't be true, it can't be true, there must be some mistake . . . Harry, my Harry, killed! I have torn the message—I didn't mean to. Why are these people looking at me so strangely?

I must get out of here—get away—I don't care where . . . It can't be true . . . Harry lying dead, burnt, it is all too horrible! I can't breathe . . . At last I have escaped, it is cooler out here . . . Oh, Harry, my Harry! Where am I to go?

What am I to do. Why couldn't I have died, too? The laughing Linda in his pocket must have been burnt, and the little gold aeroplane, that has crashed with him.

I feel faint . . . I don't know where I have walked to, I have never been in this street before . . . I have an awful feeling that I am going to collapse . . . It is silly, of course, I am not in an aeroplane that is burning . . . I will try and get a drink in here . . .

I feel better now, not so faint. I don't think port was the thing I ought to have had, but I couldn't remember what else I wanted . . .

I will have another drink before I go home, I have got

to get back to the flat sometime, back to where Harry and I were so happy together . . .

Never any more, Harry is not coming home and I shan't marry him and we will never have a tiny house or go to Devonshire again . . .

Funny, isn't it, that fire can burn you up like that. Harry who was so strong, his big shoulders, his strong arms, they are all burnt—and it's me that's left behind. I said that to him once, didn't I?

Linda's left behind—this Linda—not the laughing Linda, that's burnt in his pocket . . .

Why does that man keep saying:

"Time, gentlemen, please." . . . Time for what? Oh, I know, I must go home—I must go home . . .

It's raining—Raining lots of rain . . . Rain ought to put out fire. Perhaps if it had rained on Harry's aeroplane it would have put out the fire . . . That's a joke—rain putting out burning aeroplane . . .

I will tell Harry that . . . Splash! Splash! Splash on the pavement—and I am all wet . . . Poor Linda, so wet and so cold, she is such a long way from home and she's so tired . . .

If Harry came along in his big car he would pick me up and run me home . . . safe and home . . . home and safe . . .

Oh, what a long way it is . . . Why doesn't Harry come?

There is something on that poster . . . What is it? . . . *Harry Rumford dead!* . . . It is not true—damn you it is not true—tear it up—stamp on it—it's a lie! . . .

Harry Rumford is not dead . . . I don't believe it . . . Oh, God, it is true! . . . What am I doing here? . . . Why am I so wet?

Oh, Harry, Harry!

This nice man has got me a taxi and I haven't got any money. Yes I have. Here's ten shillings. Is that what I ought to give him?

Oh, Harry! Harry is dead!

REFLECTION TWENTY-SEVEN

I can't think. I don't know what everybody is talking about. The only thing that is going to make me feel any better is drink—I know that makes one forget.

I don't know how I got home last night. I must have walked. My shoes were still soaking this morning, and so were my clothes which were lying in the middle of the room just where I had thrown them.

I am not going to cry. I don't want to. I sent the housekeeper's boy out for the papers and he brought them back to me and everyone of them had pictures of Harry.

It is all like a dream, so perhaps it is all a dream. The pictures are not like him, they are all blurry. I am not going to look at them. I am going to drink a lot of brandy and then I am going to get up and go to the shop.

I do feel queer. Perhaps that is because of last night. I remember leaving the Savoy, but I don't know what happened then.

Harry is dead! I cried when Bessie died, and yet I am not crying about Harry. I just don't feel it is true. I don't believe I could feel anything any more.

Someone talked about death once. Yes, it was Harry. He said: "To die would be an awfully big adventure!"

But what about me? I'm not dead. There is no adventure about it. I am quite calm. It is extraordinary how calm I am, I think it is rather wonderful.

Perhaps I am just one of those people who don't feel things very deeply. Some people are made like that, they just don't feel anything.

I used to feel things. What a long time ago it seems. In Devonshire, where I used to lie about on the sands and Harry said to me:

"Do you love me, Linda?"

"I don't know," I answered, teasing him.

Then he picked me up in his arms and carried me into the water. I wasn't in my bathing-dress, so of course, I screamed and told him to put me down.

"Say you love me, then," he said.

And I wouldn't even though he threatened to throw me in clothes and all.

"You are a horrible little icicle," he said at last.

Then he dumped me down on the sands, and he ran away miles and miles away down the beach.

I tore after him panting and shouting, but I couldn't catch him, so I sat down hot and breathless, almost in tears, until he came back to me.

"Are you sorry?" he asked.

"I love you! I love you! I love you!" I said, and we just flew into each others arms and everything was all right.

I loved Harry then, with such wonderful feelings! Now he is dead I can't feel anything. I can't catch him . . . I can't . . .

Oh, this brandy is fiery, it goes right down inside one. It makes me feel steady and calm.

REFLECTION TWENTY-EIGHT

Oh, God! I have got a headache—I have never had such a headache!

There is something going to happen to-day, I wonder what it is? I was dreaming of Harry—that he would be home again soon—but he won't—he is never coming home again—he is dead!

Oh, I feel so ill and sick. I wonder why? Something happened yesterday. Why can't I remember what it was. My brain is all asleep, like cotton-wool, and my head hurts terribly.

In a moment I have got to get up, pull back the curtains and go to the shop . . . Oh, I remember now, I haven't got to go to the shop to-day—we arranged that yesterday and I said I wasn't going back to the shop . . .

Now why? I wish I could remember things! I wish I could go to sleep and go on dreaming of Harry. How my head hurts! I wonder if that champagne we had last night was corked. No, I should have noticed it, I expect.

I have got something to do to-day. I promised something yesterday. What was it I promised? I know it was very important, because I said to myself at the time:

"This is a very important thing I am doing."

But it doesn't matter, and afterwards we all drank a lot of brandy to celebrate. I know it was an important thing because someone kept saying to me:

"You will never regret this, I promise you, you will never regret it," and then we had some more brandy. How hot my hands are . . .

I must get up . . . I must get up. But I don't think my head will come off the pillow. There is something very important for me to do to-day.

I can see something white lying over that chair—I wonder what it is? It's white and . . . and something round the hem? I know! It's the white and silver dress. Of course, I wore it last night.

It was a very merry party and we danced and we drank and then we all came home in Pimples' car.

I remember something else too, I remember Pimples saying:

"Where is your sapphire ring, Linda?"

And I answered:

"It's in pawn!"

I wonder if he was angry, I can't remember what he said after that. I don't believe I meant to tell him where it was, anyway I did.

I remember saying: "It's in pawn!" and everyone laughed and I suppose they thought it was a joke.

There is someone opening the door. I wonder who it is? It's Cleone. I will tell her about my headache and she will give me a glass of brandy and I needn't get up.

She is pulling back the curtains. Dear, Cleone, it is nice of her to come and see me!

REFLECTION TWENTY-NINE

What am I doing? Stop! I must stop. I can't do this. I must be mad.

What a funny face the parson has got—and he is quite bald. I wonder why we are being married in church. Really I didn't mean to get married. I must stop it . . . I can't now because he is praying.

I don't want to marry Pimples. How awful he looks! He is fidgeting nervously with his tie.

I can't think why Mr. Cantaloupe wanted to give me away. Nobody told me he was going to, and when Cleone and I got out of the taxi, he rushed forward and made me take his arm, and here we are up the aisle.

I don't know anything about it, I don't know who made all these arrangements. I suppose as Mr. Cantaloupe has lent me this blue and fox get-up, he thought he had better come and see I didn't spoil it.

I can't remember if I made up my face. I suppose I must have, Cleone would have seen to that.

How the parson does drone on!

I don't want to marry Pimples. I wonder if I said:

"Please . . ." No, I mustn't say that—please sounds like a schoolgirl . . . just *Stop*, would they stop?

It would be awful if they took no notice and I said:

"Stop! Stop!" and the parson still went on praying and nobody took any notice.

What a funny time to get married. Why so early in the morning? I didn't want to get married anyway. I didn't know I was going to. It was only after I started to get up and had some brandy that Cleone said:

"You will be late if you don't hurry."

"Late for what?" I asked.

And then she told me.

"That's what I have been trying to remember—what I was doing to-day."

"You are a goose, Linda!" she said. "But I think you are doing the right thing."

Then we both had a glass of brandy to drink my health.

I wish Pimples wouldn't fidget so, he never could stand still. Now the parson is asking him something—if he will have me as his wife—

"Belinda Mary . . ." My name is a funny one! Belinda Mary . . . but I am not going to marry him—I will not marry him. I shall just say:

"No, I Belinda Mary won't . . ."

But now I can't say it . . . I am saying:

"I will."

I can hear myself—and it's not me. I don't want to marry him!

REFLECTION THIRTY

Well, it is done. I am married. And the Butler said:
"I have put your suitcase in behind, My Lady."

Fancy, I am Lady Glaxly, not Belinda Mary Snell—it just makes me giggle to think about it. It is so silly.

Linda Glaxly is what I shall have to sign myself in future. I wish I hadn't got such a tight feeling in my head and my chest.

Mummy was crying at the wedding. I can't think why. I was surprised to see her.

"How did you get here?" I said.

"No thanks to you, Miss!" she answered. "If I hadn't happened to see it in the *Evening Standard* last night, I would never have known—ungrateful child you are! And then that nice lady as lives near you told me what time it was taking place and so here I am!"

And I gave her a big hug for I really was pleased to see her, and then she gave me two or three big kisses and insisted on kissing Pimples too, who seemed a bit surprised.

I didn't see any of his family there. I wonder why Lady Marigold didn't come.

We are going to Paris first, and then to the south of

France. I wonder why people go to Paris for their honeymoon?

We shall be late for the boat at Folkestone if we don't hurry. We have got to be there in plenty of time so as to get the car on board.

Pimples looks very pink in the face and he is driving very fast. I suppose we shall be late if he doesn't hurry. He is an idiot.

When we got into the vestry he said: "My wife at last!" like the hero in a melodrama, and he kissed me.

Then everybody kissed me, including Mr. Cantaloupe, which was the last thing I expected from him.

All the girls from the shop were there and they all brought their friends.

I can't think why we had to get married in such a hurry. I suppose Pimples was frightened that I would change my mind if he didn't rush me into it.

The joke is it was such a rush I didn't know I was going to get married.

Why am I married to Pimples? Harry has only been dead two days and I am married to someone else. Why? I don't know why!

It is because I don't care, it is because I am drunk. I must stop Pimples, I must speak to him. I will just wait until we have passed this car. There is not really room for three cars on a road like this.

God! Look out—where are you going?—look out!!

Oh, Harry! . . .

138

REFLECTION THIRTY-ONE

I have been here a month—it seems incredible because I don't remember anything about the first three weeks. The first morning that I thought clearly and remembered what had happened I asked:

"Nurse, how long have I been here?"

"Twenty-one days to-day," she said, and for a moment I thought she must be joking, and then she added:

"You have been very ill, Lady Glaxly."

"Because of the accident?" I questioned.

"That and a touch of pneumonia," she answered. "But don't talk now, try and go to sleep if you can."

My arm is still in bandages, but the cut on my forehead is healing up beautifully, and the bruises on my tummy are beginning to fade.

Yesterday I began to feel myself again. I felt hungry too, which, as the nurse says, is always a good sign, and I began to ask all sorts of questions about what had happened, and where Pimples was.

The Nurse would not answer my questions, and so this morning I insisted on seeing the doctor, and at last I got the truth out of him.

He is a very nice man—Scotch—and the nurse tells me

that no specialist in the world could have done more for me than he did. I was brought in with a broken arm, and with a high temperature which developed into pneumonia.

They thought I must have got wet at some time and caught an internal chill which had not been looked after.

Pimples on the other hand, was only suffering from slight concussion and a few quite minor scratches.

We hit the car on my side, and I can't remember anything about the accident except screaming just as we crashed.

It was lucky this hospital was nearby or I might have bled to death, and what is luckier still is that there was such a brilliant man as Dr. Macgregor in charge.

He is rather short-sighted, and when I asked him about what had happened he stood blinking at me through his glasses, and there was rather an embarrassing silence for a few moments.

Then I realized that something was up and that he was nervous.

"I want the truth, Dr. Macgregor," I said. "I am quite strong enough this morning—really I am—to hear anything, whatever it may be. I ate an enormous breakfast, nurse will tell you, and I slept all night—so out with it!"

"It is terribly unfortunate, Lady Glaxly," he answered, "terribly unfortunate, and I regret, in some degree, that it is my fault."

"What is your fault?" I asked anxiously.

"Well, it is like this," he said at last, clearing his throat, "you were brought in on a stretcher, and, of course, we had no idea who you were. I am afraid I don't read the papers every day—I don't have time.

"You became very delirious and called out over and over again for someone—and I thought, perhaps very stupidly, that it was your husband you wanted.

"So I went to him and found he was more shaken than hurt, and that the few scratches he had were not in the slightest degree serious.

"I told you he kept calling for him, and, of course, his first idea was to see you and to soothe you if he could.

"It is quite a usual thing in my profession to find that people in an agitated state are quietened by the presence of the person they want . . . and so I brought him into your room."

I gave a little laugh—I couldn't help it.

"Poor Pimples!" I said. "I was calling for Harry, wasn't I?"

Dr. Macgregor nodded.

"You were, and you kept on talking about some place at the sea where you had been with him . . . living again the time you had spent together. I realised immediately what I had done, and I insisted upon Lord Glaxly coming away.

"But I am afraid the mischief was done—he was terribly upset. Then he told me who he was and I communicated with his relatives at once."

"Did they come here?" I asked.

"They did," answered Dr. Macgregor, "and if you will forgive me speaking bluntly, Lady Glaxly, to tell you the truth they seemed very upset about the wedding . . . but I expect you knew that."

"No, I didn't," I said, "in fact I remember very little about my wedding. I think I must have been mad at the time, anyway I was drunk. Well, I do seem to have got myself into a mess. Did Pim . . . my husband, leave any message for me?"

"He left a letter," Dr. Macgregor answered. "I was to give it to you when you were well enough. And his father, Lord Marland, has paid your bill here every week up to date."

"That is kind of the old boy," I said. "May I have the letter? It is not going to upset me, don't worry."

Rather hesitatingly Dr. Macgregor produced it from his pocket. It was written in Pimples' round untidy hand, which I know so well; it obviously was written in haste, possibly in the frenzy of the moment before his family took him away.

"I realize now what a fool I have been, and that you were with Harry Rumford the day I turned up at the Sloop Inn. I have got nothing to say about it except the sooner we get free again the better. Will you please communicate with me through your solicitors when you are well enough.

Yours,
Glaxly."

141

The signature made me smile. Pimples trying to be dignified was even more ludicrous than Pimples adoring and lovelorn.

Of course, I see that he is absolutely justified in any attitude he wishes to take up, although I can't help feeling that it was his fault for rushing and marrying me, when as far as I can make out I was not in any fit state to decide anything for myself.

I must have had a high temperature all the time, besides the fact that I was drinking myself silly and quite incapable of coping with anything after the shock of Harry's death.

I am ashamed of myself. The awful thing is I know how terribly Harry would have despised me for letting myself get in such a state. He wouldn't have done it.

Oh, Harry! Harry!...

REFLECTION THIRTY-TWO

I seem to have become quite a famous person—not over-night as the poets did, but over six weeks.

The press mentioned me occasionally in a very condescending way when I was Linda Snell, but now I am quite celebrated.

Nurse let me have the back papers when I was well enough, with the pictures and decriptions of my accident. Pimples and I were headlines for nearly three days!

The problem is how am I going to live. I am not a bit anxious to apply to Pimples for any money, but I can't work for at least another month. I have got to rest for two or three hours every day and be awfully careful of my arm.

Another blow which has upset me is find that Cleone has been sent down to Monte Carlo for a fortnight to show Cantaloupe's clothes and she won't be back until the last week of September.

This gives me eight days here alone not knowing who is in London or where my next meal is coming from.

I haven't got a penny in the world so I suppose the only thing is, to find out what I can pawn. There are two or three fox collars on my Spring coats, but I don't suppose they will fetch much.

Then, lastly, there is Harry's ring, but I would do anything before I would part with that.

I wish photographers would give one free meals instead of free sittings, that would be far more useful.

So here I am, in just the same plight I was in months ago when I first came to London. What is worse, I owe two months' rent on the flat, and that isn't a pleasant thing to contemplate.

REFLECTION THIRTY-THREE

I am not angry, I am just surprised.

If I had thought about it beforehand seriously, I suppose I should have realised that Pimple's family would have been horrified at the idea of his marrying me.

I did think that Lady Marigold though would have been either indifferent or else sympathetic with Pimples if not with me. But she is just as furious as her parents are.

She came round to see me yesterday, unannounced. I had been feeling rather rotten and was lying down on my bed resting when there came a knock on the door. I called out "Come in," thinking it was a messenger or the housekeeper.

To my surprise in walked my sister-in-law.

"How do you do? How lovely it is to see you!" I said, getting up.

I was so lonely and had been longing to have someone to talk to. But my sister-in-law was a very different woman from the gay, laughing, cocktail-drinking person of but a few weeks ago.

"I want to have a serious talk with you," she said.

"All right," I answered, getting off the bed and clearing

some of my clothes out of the chair so that she could sit down.

There was an awkward pause and then she said:

"It is very unfortunate that you should have gone off and got married in this hurry. Pimples has no money, you know."

"I know that," I answered, "but I didn't marry your brother for money . . . in fact, I didn't mean to marry him at all."

"In which case it is very unfortunate that you did," Lady Marigold said grimly.

I could see she didn't believe me.

"I have come here," Lady Marigold went on, "to propose that some legal compromise may be reached, and my parents suggest that you meet them at a solicitor's office."

"All right," I said, "if that is what Pimples wants."

Now I have got enough of Mummy in me to hate being bullied. I don't know why, but the moment people try to do me down it makes me absolutely furious. If they are pleasant and nice, I am as weak as water.

So when the solicitor started in a hectoring tone I listened for a moment and then I said:

"Look here, I am not going to be talked to like this! I am perfectly prepared to listen to what you have to say and I will agree to any reasonable proposition you make, but there is no getting away from the fact that I am married to Lord Glaxly, and that I am his wife.

"You can't make out that I am a baby-snatcher for I am not yet nineteen and he is twenty-five, so that line of talk is just nonsense and you know it!"

The little man seemed somewhat taken aback by this, and he gave a quick look at Lord and Lady Marland as if to say:

"There, what can I do with such a common creature?"

But the old boy spoke then, and I must say he is a gentleman with a charming manner and a decent way of speaking. In fact, if he wasn't my father-in-law, I am sure I should like him very much.

"Perhaps," he said quietly, "you will tell us what you suggest is to be done about this very unfortunate marriage. Our son has no wish to see you again and I gather that you are of the same mind."

"That is quite right, I am," I answered. "I don't suppose

you will believe me—but I didn't want to marry your son —it has all been a terrible mistake and the sooner we all get out of it the better."

At that the solicitor and the old man put their heads together and talked for a long time in hushed voices. Then they tried to explain to me the legal points, but I must say I got rather muddled with them.

As far as I can make out an annulment would be the easiest course—but it takes a year, and as they are anxious to rescue their precious little son from my toils immediately, they have come to the conclusion that a divorce is best.

"That is all very well," I said, "but who is going to be divorced?"

As I expected, they wanted me to be the guilty party. I don't mind very much, and in a way I feel it is up to me to get out of this mess. At the same time I can't think of anyone whom I could possibly be divorced for.

They were so pleased at my not being horrified at the idea, that they offered me £1000 on the day that I gave them the evidence.

That offer gave me courage to ask for something in the meantime, although I felt awful at doing it.

"The moment I am well enough, I will get a job," I said. "Please don't think I want your money—it is just that for a little while I am not in a fit state to work."

This led to another whispered conversation, and, of course, I could see what was worrying them. If they paid me so much a month I mightn't be in any hurry to give them the evidence they wanted! However, after a little while, the solicitor turned to me:

"I have to tell you that Lord Glaxly has no private income of his own, he is on an allowance, and if you go to the law as his legal wife for support, Lord Marland will cut him off with a shilling and you will be unable to obtain any relief from him whatsoever.

"However, as we are sure that you have no desire to drive Lord Marland to take up this attitude or to invite any further publicity, we are agreeable that until you furnish us with evidence you will receive the sum of three pounds a week paid regularly into your bank.

"Should you make an endeavour to have this increased, Lord Marland will undertake no further responsibility on

147

your behalf and merely cease paying his son's allowance until the marriage is dissolved."

I saw that they had me on toast whatever I did, but I was so glad to get any money at all that I agreed.

Feeling rather like a discharged kitchen-maid I walked out into the street, and only when I got back to the flat did I feel like crying. I suppose it is their son and they mind frightfully that he has married the daughter of an acrobat.

REFLECTION THIRTY-FOUR

It is all very well, but I don't believe that one can go backwards.

At one time I thought three pounds a week was a luxury. Now I find it is the worst type of poverty. It is Autumn and I can't go on for ever walking out in the wind in a thin *crêpe de Chine* dress and pretending it's too hot for a coat.

I am only praying that I shall find some sort of work soon.

Thank goodness Hugh is back. When I told him what had happened, he was most awfully nice and understanding.

"Poor Linda," he said, "you *have* got yourself into a mess."

And when I told him about the divorce he was horrified.

"I don't see why you should do all the dirty work," he grumbled. "Pimples has only himself to blame. Let him be the guilty party."

"I shan't get a penny of money if I do," I said. "I can't live on air, Hugh."

"You will when old Marland dies," he answered. "He is

bound to leave his son everything and then you would certainly get a third of his income."

"How old is he?" I asked.

"About sixty-two or sixty-three," he answered.

"So if he lives to a good ripe eighty, I starve for eighteen years! Thanks, Hugh, darling, but I don't think that piece of advice is a very good one."

"Look here, Linda . . ." Hugh started, but I stopped him, putting my fingers against his mouth.

"Don't say it, Hugh, I know what you are going to do, you are going to offer me money—and our friendship has always been such fun because we have never been the slightest bit of trouble to each other. Please don't, it might spoil everything, and I couldn't bear it."

I wouldn't let him talk about it any more, as I know how poor Hugh is. He has a tiny allowance from his father, and he is much poorer than any of his brother officers, and can't even manage to keep a car.

But it just shows that one's true friends will stand by one in trouble. Cleone and Hugh are just the dearest and sweetest people in the world.

Cleone has been absolutely marvellous and got me asked to lots of luncheon and dinner parties just because she knew I was lonely and at times hungry.

And I know, though I shall hate to take it, that she is going to give me an Autumn outfit as soon as she has saved the money.

Poor Cleone is hard up herself at the moment because, while she had a marvellous time at Monte Carlo, all expenses paid by Cantaloupe's, she was silly enough to gamble and, of course, she lost.

As she said:

"It is only the rich who win because they don't care; money is magnetised by indifference."

Cleone has got a new boy friend, and I really believe that she is beginning to fall in love again.

I do hope so, because I would like her to be awfully happy. He is awfully nice, although he has not got a lot of money.

He is secretary and general factotum to Sir Sydney Wrex, a very rich North Country business magnate.

Norman Vaughan—that is Cleone's young man's name—goes everywhere with Sir Sydney and manages so many of his affairs that I think he must be indispensable.

In which case they could easily get married, but Cleone is rather a secretive person and she won't tell me what her real feelings are. But there is a new light in her eyes and she seems awfully happy when Norman calls.

They both like the same things and they sit for hours discussing the latest book or going to concerts at the Queen's Hall.

I have been out with them two or three times and I like Norman, but he is serious-minded, and I must admit that if I had always to be with him I should find him a little dull.

But Cleone thinks he is brilliant, and if you admire a man enough I believe that is half-way to being in love with him.

REFLECTION THIRTY-FIVE

Cleone is engaged. I am so pleased.

She is awfully happy, but they are going to wait at least three months before they get married.

Anyway, until after Christmas, because Christmas is such a busy time for Sir Sydney Wrex, and Norman will have too much to do looking after him then to marry Cleone.

Cleone is quite a different person these days. She has stopped being sad and languid and looks healthier and more alive.

She is rushing around buying things for her trousseau whenever she has an odd moment from Cantaloupe's.

The thing that pleases Cleone most of all is that they are going to live in the country.

Sir Sydney has heaps of houses, but the one he spends most of his time at is in Cheshire, and he has offered Norman a small house on the estate, only a mile or two from "Five Oaks," the big house.

I can't help feeling a little jealous of Cleone and Norman, they are so in love—just like Harry and I were. Norman reminds me of Harry in some ways, especially when he is looking after Cleone.

He treats her as if she were made of china. It rather depresses me at times to think that if I happened to break my ankle or hurt my thumb with a hammer, no-one would care.

I suppose it is too much to expect that I shall ever find anyone as wonderful as Harry again.

I don't think things in life ever happen twice, so I suppose for the rest of my life I shall find myself putting up with second best, and liking it, I expect, as time goes on.

REFLECTION THIRTY-SIX

Yesterday morning I was lying in bed thinking how pleasant it was that I hadn't got to get up and rush to the shop, when the door opened and Cleone came in.

The moment I saw her face I knew something terrible had happened.

"What is the matter?" I asked, sitting up quickly.

She sat down on the edge of my bed and held out a letter for me to read.

I thought at first Norman must have chucked her, or that he was killed or something, but when I read the letters I realised that all these fears were groundless.

It wasn't Norman, it was Cleone's first husband who was the trouble.

I had really forgotten all about him. Cleone had never spoken to me about that part of her life, and I imagined that the other girls at the shop were right and that either she was never married to him at all, or else he must be dead.

The truth is entirely different. The Count di Rivoli—what a theatrical-sounding name!—is very much alive and still married to Cleone.

She really thought that he was dead as she had not heard

from him for several years. But instead he is living in Italy in some obscure village and growing violets or something like that.

The only cheerful news is that he is undoubtedly living in sin with a very pretty Italian actress, and Cleone may be able to divorce him.

Then Cleone, who I had always known so controlled, so sane and sensible, broke down and cried bitterly.

I didn't know what to do to comfort her, and of course, I cried too—I always do when I see tears in someone else's eyes, even at a film or on the stage.

It did seem the most awful bad luck.

"Don't darling," I kept saying, "don't, Cleone—I am sure it will come out all right."

And, of course, I pray it will for her sake.

REFLECTION THIRTY-SEVEN

The day started off badly with great troubles about money.

Pimples' solicitors have stopped paying me anything and although Mr. Church has gone to the Courts, apparently it takes months to get a case heard.

. It all seems to me very odd and troublesome, but I don't like to say too much because it upsets Hugh, who insisted on my going to see Mr. Church.

I am sure their ideas are right and this is all for the best, but I wonder how they expect me to pay the rent, buy a new pair of shoes, save up for new clothes and have my hair washed (which, after all, is a necessity) all on nothing a week?

This morning I was wondering about it as I dressed and wishing I could get a job, when they sent up from downstairs to say there was someone to see me.

I said they could come up, and to my surprise a small shabby little woman arrived.

She was wrinkled and withered, rather like a little brown apple, but she had the brightest blue eyes, and I couldn't think who she reminded me of until she told me she was Bessie's mother.

Of course I was thrilled; I asked her to sit down and made her a cup of tea on my gas ring, and we had a long talk and a good cry together.

She was a perfect darling, very shy and quiet. She lives with her husband in Wales, he is a jobbing gardener when he is in work.

She told me how horrified they both were when Bessie went on the stage. They would have been still more horrified if they had known the truth about their daughter's life.

I soon realised that Bessie had never said a word to her mother about men and Mrs. Evans kept saying:

"Father never did like Bessie going on the stage—we have always been respectable, you see."

The poor dear had only just heard about Bessie's death. It had been in some of the London papers at the time and it got copied into their local one, which even then was months old before a neighbour showed her what news it contained.

I told her that Bessie had strained her inside and that was why she had to have an operation. She was very worried about it and kept saying:

"Such a strong child she was, Miss, you wouldn't believe how boney she was at eight or nine. She won prizes at our local show and the neighbours were always congratulating us on our Bessie."

After a second cup of tea, she told me of the awful struggle they had had lately.

Bessie's father had been out of work for a long time, and even when he got the chance of a job his rheumatism was so bad that he often had to refuse because he could hardly move.

So the poor old lady went "charing" but it was hard work, especially with an ailing husband on her hands.

I said to Mrs. Evans:

"Bessie has left money and I know she meant it for you."

The old woman was quite overcome.

I put on my hat and coat and we went along there and then to the Bank; I explained the whole thing to the manager, and, of course, he let me have the money, and when Mrs. Evans realised how much it was she nearly fainted with surprise.

"How could our Bessie have saved all that?" she asked.

"She was a very good actress," I told her, "they thought very highly of her on the stage. And she was always saving for you and her father."

I told a lot more lies of that sort and I have never seen anyone as happy as that old woman was.

"A hundred pounds!" she whispered, over and over again, "a hundred pounds—it's a fortune."

Finally, we went out to the cemetery by Underground and I showed her Bessie's grave and we put flowers on it.

Then I gave her some food and saw her off on the Cardiff Express, still whispering to herself:

"One hundred pounds—just fancy our Bessie saving all that!"

It was only as the train steamed out of the station that I remembered that I should have lunched with Norman and Cleone.

I had forgotten everything about them and I felt rather guilty, so I went to a telephone box and rang Cleone's number—there was no reply.

So I thought the best thing I could do was to go myself to Cressaway House and see if I could find Norman.

Norman has a comfortable office there and I knew Cleone often went to him when she left the shop; waited for him to finish his work so that they could go out to dinner together.

Cressaway House is an enormous mansion, and the moment one rings the front door bell one is aware that the whole house absolutely smells of money.

Sir Sydney Wrex is rolling, but everyone tells us that he is mean and hard and won't give a penny to charity or anything like that.

Norman admires Sir Sydney very much because he is so clever, but, at the same time, he says sometimes he is quite brutal to his work-people or those he employs personally.

Of course his story is rather a sad one, so one could make allowances for him, but even so it seems unnecessary to acquire a reputation for being so sharp in business and close-fisted.

When Sir Sydney was a young man he married a beautiful girl belonging to a very good family.

It was considered, I believe, at the time a brilliant marriage for him because, though he was a promising young man and already making a certain amount of money, his parents were only working people while his wife had always been in Society. They got married.

A year later she went off her head and was shut up in a lunatic asylum.

It was only then that he learnt that there was insanity in the family, and that if her parents had behaved decently they would never have allowed her to marry anyone.

All this happened years ago, but she is still alive. Norman says that Sir Sydney pays thousands a year for her upkeep, for she is not in an ordinary asylum, but in a sort of glorified nursing home where they charge exorbitant prices.

It seems terrible bad luck that he has no one to inherit his colossal fortune, which is one of the largest in England.

Having heard all this about Sir Syndey I took a special interest in the house. To my mind it is hideous, much too ornate and grand.

There is a great black-and-white marble staircase carpeted in a hideous shade of red, and the windows are all hung with curtains be-tasselled and draped in the fashion of pre-war days.

There are great pictures everywhere, mostly religious, but one in the hall was of a very beautiful woman.

I felt that must be Sir Sydney's wife, but I didn't have time to stop and look as I was following the butler through to Norman's room.

We walked down panelled passages, all rather dark and gloomy, and I thought it was enough to make anyone disagreeable living all alone in this pompous house with too many liveried servants.

When we got to Norman's room he was not there, and the butler said:

"If you will wait a moment, madam, I will find out if Mr. Vaughan is with Sir Sydney."

When the door opened, I thought it was the butler returning, but in came a tall figure with steely grey eyes, heavy eyebrows and dark hair.

Of course I knew at once that it must be Sir Sydney, and I must say, in a way, he is very good looking. The correct expression is, I think, a strong face.

That really does express his square jaw, determined mouth and rather frightening eyes.

He was also much younger than I expected. One always thinks of a tycoon as being very old.

He speaks in a sharp, somewhat staccato fashion which makes him very authoratative.

"You want Vaughan?" he said to me, abruptly.

"It is not important," I answered, "if he is busy."

"He is," Sir Sydney replied, "and I shall require him for at least another two hours."

"Then I won't wait," I said, "I only called on the chance that he was free."

"Who are you?" Sir Sydney said sharply, "you are not the girl he is engaged to?"

"No, I am not," I replied, "but I am a great friend of hers."

"And your name?" Sir Sydney asked.

"Linda Glaxly," I answered, feeling rather like a prisoner being cross examined.

"Glaxly . . . ?" he said. "How do I know that name?"

I felt certain that he had seen some reference to my marriage in the papers, but I didn't enlighten him.

"Perhaps you know my father-in-law, Lord Marland," I said demurely.

"Marland—of course I do—I am on a couple of companies with him. So you are the girl his son has married. Well, how do you get on with him?"

"With whom?" I questioned, "father or son?"

"Either," Sir Sydney said.

"I don't," I replied, feeling rather like an impudent puppy talking to a growling mastiff.

At my answer there was just the faintest suspicion of a smile at the corner of his mouth, and I knew then my answer had amused him.

Norman had told me that he was famous for his blunt speech, and I felt that if he liked frankness I could be just as frank as he was likely to be and his next remark gave me an opportunity.

"Well, I won't keep you," he said, "I hope we shall meet again some time."

"Why?" I said, looking at him with wide open eyes.

"Why?" he echoed, obviously a little taken aback. "Oh, I expect you would like to tell me your life story, I have listened to it from most dis-illusioned young women."

"And that makes you more cynical than ever, I suppose," I said quietly.

"Who says I am cynical," asked Sir Sydney, "who told you that, eh?"

"A great many people," I said gently, "that is why I should never attempt to enlist your sympathy, I promise you that."

"You do, do you?" he said reflectively, looking at me in a more interested way.

"Well, I mustn't keep you," I said, holding out my hand. "I have enjoyed meeting you—you are much nicer than I thought you would be."

That remark surprised him more than ever, and I could see that he was considering what else he would say to me, and then following me into the passage.

"What do you think of my house?" he asked.

"It is very gloomy," I replied, "and much too grand."

"You don't mind saying what you think, do you?" he said, in tones of surprise.

"I have always heard that North Country people liked plain speaking," I answered.

"So they do—so they do," Sir Sydney said.

"But perhaps you would rather I was complimentary," I suggested.

"I never said so," he answered sharply, "I like the truth. Why do you think the house is gloomy?"

"Well, don't you think it is?" I asked wide-eyed.

But he didn't answer my question. Instead he said:

"You had better come and dine with me. What are you doing to-morrow night?"

"I should like to," I said, "I am doing nothing very exciting."

"Eight o'clock sharp, then," he said abruptly.

And without another word, not even "Good-bye" he turned and walked away as a footman sprang out of the shadows from nowhere and opened the door for me.

Outside in the street I felt as though I had escaped from a den of lions, but at the same time I am rather excited at the thought of dining with him.

He certainly is an interesting personality, and it will be fun to make him look surprised at what I say.

Obviously most people who meet him are terrified and I feel that even Norman is in a blue funk in case he

REFLECTION THIRTY-EIGHT

Good resolutions don't always come off—at least not mine, and I don't expect I am any different from other people.

Anyway, when I dined with Sir Sydney tonight—which is the third time—I told him the story of my life, in spite of what I had said. But he did ask me to.

I had never expected to be asked to dine again after the first time. That was a dreadful dinner.

We sat stiffly in the huge dining-room with four servants to wait on us and the food was brought in on silver dishes which seemed too big for what they contained.

I suppose Sir Sydney has got so used to living alone that he had never noticed that the dining-room looks exactly like a mausoleum.

If someone had told me there was a corpse upstairs I should not have been in the least surprised.

Of course, feeling like that, I couldn't be a bit amusing. The only thing was to make my host talk, and that I managed to do fairly well.

I have always heard that a successful woman lets a man do all the talking, and I suppose by that it means success where a man she doesn't love is concerned.

If you love someone there are such lots of things you want to say. Hundreds of facts you want to find out about them and there seem endless topics of conversation.

When Harry was with me there was never a moment when there weren't a million things I wanted to say.

By the end of dinner Sir Sydney was telling me all about his factories and how he had started as a boy at 8s. a week.

"What do you do with your money now?" I asked, and he looked at me in a surprised way.

"Do?" he questioned.

"Well, you obviously can't spend all you make," I said, "even though you have got several houses."

"Only fools spend all they make," he growled at me.

"Don't say you are saving for a rainy day," I laughed.

"And why not?" he asked.

"Because you couldn't have a very rainy day now," I replied.

"Everyone can," he replied, "if we have another trade slump . . ."

"Yes, yes," I interrupted, "but you couldn't be really poor, not like you were when you were a boy. You might have to give up one of your houses or sacrifice the silver plate, but you wouldn't have to go without—as you have been telling me—without your boots and not know where your next meal is coming from."

"In other words you are urging me to be extravagant," he said.

"I am asking you to spend and be happy," I replied. "There's a nice slogan for you, anyway!"

It seemed to tickle him, my idea that by spending more money he could have a better time.

I have never seen anyone have apparently less fun out of their money.

I don't think he enjoys himself at all and I believe that fundamentally he is lonely, and his gruff manner is because he has a grudge against people who seem to be getting more out of life than he is.

Norman told me that he had a bad temper, and the second time I dined with him he stormed at his poor butler because he brought the wrong brandy.

The butler was terrified, I could see that. But bad temper does not frighten me—not Sir Sydney's sort anyway, because he reminds me of a dog barking fiercely and at the same time being unable to bite anybody.

When the butler had gone shaking from the room, he said:

"He is a good servant, Keen, but a damned fool."

"Do you pay him extra not to mind when you are disagreeable?" I asked.

He glared at me, then he laughed, and was in a much better temper for the rest of the evening.

To-night when I dined with him I insisted on going out to a restaurant, I really couldn't stand the mausoleum any longer, and so we had a very good dinner at Claridge's.

Rather formal, and there were not many people there, but I really believe that Sir Sydney enjoyed himself. He did try to grumble at the food and the wine, but I said:

"Nonsense! You can't do that when you are out with me!"

To my surprise he agreed that the cooking was really excellent after all and that the wine was not so bad.

During dinner he asked me about Pimples and then after that I had to tell him exactly what had happened to me. He was frightfully interested and asked me about everything so I told him about Harry.

"I don't expect you to believe that we weren't really lovers," I said.

"Why shouldn't I?" he answered. "You don't look like a liar to me."

"No one else would believe me," I said, "so that is why I've let them think what they like."

"Most people are fools," Sir Sydney remarked.

There was a silence, then he went on:

"I suppose you think you will never love anyone again."

"Not in exactly the same way," I answered, "but I hope one day I will fall in love because it's such a wonderful feeling and I'm afraid of being lonely and miserable the rest of my life.

"I was thinking of Cleone and how she had found happiness after years of having an aching heart for Peter."

"You'll fall in love," Sir Sydney said, "and be just as silly the next time."

But he said it kindly. Then he asked me lots of questions. I think that clever people are often genuinely interested in other people's lives.

Of course he found out how hard up I was, and I told

him that I wanted to get a job and I asked him if he could suggest anything.

"In another month," I said, "I shall be able to go back to Cantaloupe's, my arm is practically all right. Or do you think I ought to try the stage again?"

"Can you act?" he asked.

"Oh, yes, I can," I assured him. "I believe I should be very good if I had the chance."

"Every flibberty-gibbet with a pretty face thinks that," he said discouragingly.

"Do you think I am a flibberty-gibbet?" I asked.

"I expect you are like all the rest," he answered, "out for all you can get."

"Of course, I am," I replied, "and so are you. You always have been."

"That is true enough," he admitted.

"Well, what is the difference?" I asked, "except that you have been successful and I haven't?"

"There is plenty of time for you yet," Sir Sydney said dryly.

"I suppose there is," I answered, "and I suppose it is ungrateful of me to talk of failure, but I only hope that if I do fail completely, or, for that matter, if I succeed that I am not as disillusioned as you are. You are so bitter about things!"

"You talk like a fool—or a child!" he said. "You wait until you are as old as I am."

And he changed the conversation. I thought he couldn't still be unhappy about his wife, but perhaps he is. I have found out that she went mad because she was having a baby.

It seems a terrible thing that he can't get rid of her and marry someone else, but from the very beginning there has never been the slightest chance of curing her.

I told Sir Sydney about Cleone and Norman, and of course Norman hadn't told him about Cleone's husband.

"What are they going to do about it?" he asked.

I explained that they were going to try and get a divorce but that the terrible thing was that it was going to cost such a lot of money.

"Vaughan can afford it," he said, "I pay him a damned good wage."

"But they have planned every penny of that for furnish-

166

ing their house," I said. "You have no idea how much money it costs to furnish a house these days."

"What are you suggesting I do?" Sir Sydney asked.

"Well, there is Christmas coming," I replied.

I was very anxious to help Norman and Cleone, but terrified I should say something that would do Norman harm, as Sir Sydney is a very odd-tempered man.

"You are very free and easy with my money," Sir Sydney said.

"I would be free and easy with my own if I had it—that is the fun of having money, being able to give presents to everyone. It is fun having them, but it is even more exciting going out and choosing presents for people you like."

I was thinking of Harry's little gold aeroplane as I spoke.

"What do you expect me to give you for Christmas, a present?" Sir Sydney asked.

"Well, you can put my present in with Norman's if you will pay the expenses of his case," I said, wondering how he would take the idea.

"I never said I would pay for his case," Sir Sydney said.

"No, but you will, won't you?" I pleaded.

Then I put out my hand and put it on his.

"Do!" I said softly, "it will be such a snub in the eye to the people who think you are mean."

He refused to discuss the matter any more, but I have a feeling he will do it, when it comes to the point.

I told Cleone and she was thrilled, but she says she will not tell Norman just in case Sir Sydney doesn't do anything. Not that she really expects him to, anyway.

"My dear, we haven't got a hope," she said. "He has never been known to give anyone anything, let alone one of his servants. It is very sweet of you, Linda dear, but I don't mind betting that we shan't even get a Christmas card from him, let alone a present."

That has made me more determined than ever that Sir Sydney shall give Norman a present. I don't know why, but it is almost fascinating to see if I can beat Sir Sydney over this matter.

I am just determined that he shall spend money, and if

I can make him, I shall feel that I am a very clever person with lots of will power.

He is a queer character. I feel that he is concentrating on his business all the time, and that it is an awful effort for him to unbend and talk about anything else for even a few minutes.

I get the impression that he finds me amusing as long as he can remember that I am there.

But half the time I am talking I don't believe he is listening to me at all, but working out exactly what tax he will have to pay or how many orders his factory can execute between now and next year.

When I got back to-night and found a long letter from Mummy asking me what I was doing and suggesting that she could do with some cash if I had any. That's a joke, if there ever was one!

As I came back in Sir Sydney's car to-night covered with a huge sable rug, the cost of which would be my income for a year, I couldn't help wondering why rich people can't give you nice tips occasionally.

It does seem absurd that they should spend five or six pounds on your dinner and never offer you the equivalent.

It wouldn't make the slightest difference to Sir Sydney if he gave me ten pounds. I noticed to-night he left fifteen shillings on the plate, and I quite wished I could have gone halves with the waiter.

I am dreadfully hard up—I haven't even a shilling to put in the gas-meter for my fire.

I went to a photographer's this morning who I used to go to when I was at Cantaloupe's and they promised me a few sittings for advertisements later on.

There will be heaps in the New Year, but just now, Christmas time, most people have already got their advertisements out.

I simply can't do without some more clothes. Cleone was a perfect angel and gave me a dress and coat, and I managed to sell some of my summer things, which had cost pounds and pounds, for a few shillings.

My evening dresses are perfectly all right, but I can't go on much longer wearing the same dress and coat, day in and day out.

As it happens I was thinking of trying to borrow some money from Mummy, but now it doesn't seem as if it would be much use.

"I have had a bit of bad luck," she wrote, *but everything would have been all right if Bill hadn't turned nasty because I lost a few pounds racing. He has closed up and won't part. If you could oblige for a few weeks, Linda, I would be grateful."*

Poor Mummy she has got it into her head that when one has got a title one is rolling in money, and she won't see that since my accident I am even worse off than as Linda Snell.

I can't make her understand about Pimples, she just wouldn't listen.

"A man has to support his wife," she says. "You go and tell the Judge so, he will soon put your husband in his right place."

I suppose I could move into a cheaper room, but I haven't got the money to move and here they do let me owe, even though they are writing nastier letters every month threatening me with Court proceedings.

I have taken no notice of their letters so far, and although I did pay one week of Pimple's money against my account, that was only a drop in the ocean, and sooner or later there is going to be a real bust up, I can tell that.

I feel so miserable sometimes that I could sit down and cry. I go to sleep thinking of money, and I wake up thinking of it, but it seems to get me no further. I shall begin to look an old hag if I don't take care.

When I told Cleone about Bessie's mother and her money, she said:

"Why Linda, what a silly you are! You could easily have paid yourself back what you spent on the funeral."

She didn't understand when I said that I would rather die than touch a penny of that swine Teddy's money.

He killed Bessie, and if I touched his money I should feel a Judas.

REFLECTION THIRTY-NINE

Such an amazing thing has happened, that I must think it over from the very beginning and get it clear to myself.

I simply can't believe my own memory, and yet in a way it was silly not to have guessed it might happen, and if I were really clever, which I ought to be, I should have been hoping for it all along.

Lying here in bed in the dark I keep thinking that I must have dreamt it all. And yet I feel on my wrist my new diamond watch. I just can't take it off because it is so exciting to have it.

In some ways I am dreading the future, yet it is marvellous to think that I shan't have to worry any more and that the beasts who own this room can take it after to-morrow.

When I woke up this morning I realised that something horrible was going to happen.

It was raining for one thing, pouring down and everything seemed grey, gloomy and very cold.

I opened a letter which had arrived by the early post and found that it was a notice to quit. That was beastly enough, but nothing to what happened in the next hour.

I was getting dressed rather slowly feeling so depressed

that I couldn't even begin to plan what I was going to do, when there was a sharp tap on the door and a little man in a bowler hat arrived to take possession.

I stood staring at him like a fool. I could hardly believe what he told me until he came in and started taking an inventory of the furniture.

"Don't take on, lady, it is all in a day's work," he said, as I made a feeble sort of protest.

Then I felt so miserable that I just sat down and howled.

I had had no breakfast and what with the rain and everything I felt that I just couldn't cope with things.

I know it was stupid of me to give way to my feelings, but I often feel rotten in the mornings nowadays, although after I have had some food and a cup of tea the feeling wears off.

"Now don't take on," the little man kept saying, "ain't you got no one who can help you? What about a young man?"

"I don't want a young man, I want some work," I said in between my sobs.

"That's what we all want," he said. "I have got two sons on the dole, and my daughter is laid up with laryngitis on half-pay. It is hard times for all of us, Missy. But there, such a pretty girl as you ought to be able to get along all right."

He was really a terribly kind little man in spite of his profession, which must be a beastly one, always being hated wherever he goes.

In the end he put his own shilling into the gas meter and we had a cup of tea together. We must have made a ludicrous picture, it seems to me now; at the time I didn't think about it.

If anyone had come in they would have laughed.

Me in my pink and lace dressing-gown and the little man with his bowler hat firmly on his head—he never took it off—both gossiping over a cup of tea before he seized my property and threw me out into the street.

"You don't seem to have many assets," he said to me finally, after we had had a long talk about his famly, the iniquities of the dole and the difficulty of finding work.

"No, they have all gone a long time ago," I said mournfully.

"Gone to Uncle's, eh?" he said. "It's the same with our

171

things. We had to let the clock go last week, and it had been my father's and his father's before him, but as I said to the wife, 'we can do without the time, Missus, but we can't do without new boots,' so off it had to go."

He was such a funny little man with thin greying hair, a draggled moustache and pale watery eyes which looked as if he might burst into tears at any moment.

But the way he took life as it came made me feel ashamed of my outburst. After all I had only myself to look after, while he had his family and his wife.

In the end we parted the best of friends when I went out to lunch, although he locked the door on me as I wasn't allowed to take anything away except what I stood up in.

The little man and I descended the stairs together.

I paddled along in the rain holding up an umbrella, feeling that the wet was soaking through my thin shoes and knowing that it was the very worst thing I could do as the Doctor had warned me to be especially careful of getting damp.

I was just wondering if I went into the Ritz or the Berkeley and sat looking wistful if I should find someone I knew to stand me lunch, when in a block of cars at the corner of Piccadilly and Berkeley Street, I saw Sir Sydney's Rolls.

I was so desperate and so miserable and so hungry that I did a thing I should never have done in any other circumstances.

I walked through the traffic towards him, turned the handle of the door and got into the car.

Sir Sydney growled a rather surprised "Good morning" at me, but I didn't wait for him to say more, I just said:

"Please, Sir Sydney, will you give me lunch, I am starvingly hungry and I haven't got a penny in the world."

Without answering me he picked up the speaking-tube at his side and said to the chauffeur:

"Go home."

"You are wet," he said sharply, as he replaced the tube.

"Soaked," I said, "but it can't be helped. I have been turned out of my flat and so I am wandering around like a lost sheep."

"Why didn't you telephone Vaughan," he said, "he could

at least have found you a meal?"

"The telephone is cut off," I said, "and Cleone had already left for the shop, otherwise I could have borrowed something from her."

I felt so lonely and tired and everything, especially after crying, that I really couldn't bother to explain any more. I just lay back in the car until we arrived at Cressaway House.

I was really feeling a little faint, I suppose, because I only know that it was the greatest effort to get out of the car and walk into the house.

Perhaps I looked strange, for the moment we got in Sir Sydney sent for some brandy and made me drink a small glass.

"Bring luncheon for two," he said to the butler. "We will have it in the library by the fire, not in the drawing-room."

"I am afraid it will be a few moments, Sir Sydney," the butler replied, "we were not expecting you in to luncheon today."

"I am quite aware of that," Sir Sydney snapped, "be as quick as you can."

As soon as the butler had gone he made me sit in a big arm-hair by the fire and said:

"You had better take off your shoes and stockings."

I was feeling much too weak to argue and anyway my feet were absolutely soaked.

Only when my silk stockings were hanging on the small brass guard in front of a huge log fire did I realise that perhaps it was rather strange to be sitting with bare feet in the library of one of the most feared men in the business world.

I am glad I have got such nice feet, they are very white and luckily I had remembered to paint my toe-nails only two days ago.

However, Sir Sydney didn't look at me, he went to a side-table where there were all sorts of drinks and mixed a cocktail.

"Drink this," he said, bringing it to me in his hand.

When I had done as I was told I began to feel much better.

"You are a Good Samaritan," I said to him.

He grunted in reply, picked up the telephone without

answering me, cancelled his luncheon engagement in the City and any other appointments he had made until after three o'clock.

"Will the City be in an uproar," I said, "and will all the shares drop to rock bottom, or whatever they do? I feel very guilty at upsetting your arrangements like this."

"You better tell me what the trouble is," he said sharply.

I felt rather embarrassed sitting perched in the huge red leather chair with bare feet, so I slipped on to the hearthrug, and having thrown off my hat I felt it was more cosy and less formal.

Anyway I told him exactly what sort of trouble I was in. And I made my story quite amusing with descriptions of my little bailiff friend and the fact that I had nowhere to lay my head.

When I had finished Sir Sydney didn't speak for some moments.

He sat looking at me, tapping his fingers on the arm of his chair, his lower lip slightly protruding—a trick I have noticed he always has when thinking deeply about anything.

Suddenly he sprang to his feet and rang the bell. When the butler came hurrying in, he said:

"Where is luncheon—it can't take all this time?"

"It is just coming, Sir Sydney," the butler answered, apologetically.

Almost immediately two footmen appeared bringing in a small table, which they set down near the fire.

The cook must be a genius for we had the most delicious lunch and I felt all the better for it. Sydney wanted me to have some hock, but after the cocktail and the brandy I thought it wiser to refuse.

When the coffee came he lit a huge cigar and then having waved the servants away so that we were alone, he said:

"What are your plans?"

I shrugged my shoulders, only more cheerfully—I always feel much brighter about things after food.

I am quite certain that before facing any problem if people would eat and drink they would find their difficulties far less terrifying. I suppose that's a silly thought, because most people can't afford to eat and drink.

Sir Sydney's next remark came as a great surprise.

"I have got a suggestion," he said. "I am not making it on the spur of the moment—in fact I didn't intend to tell you about it just yet—however, circumstances alter cases, so I will offer you this as an alternative plan to walking about in the rain."

He got up as he spoke and stood with his back to the fire, looking at me as I sat with my legs curled underneath me in the corner of the big leather sofa.

"Well, what is it?" I asked, breaking the silence which had fallen between us.

For a moment the fierce Sir Sydney seemed to hesitate as if in embarrassment.

"What about coming to live here with me?" he said, and gave a big puff at his cigar.

I sat looking at him stupidly and suddenly I realised what he meant.

"Oh!" I ejaculated in complete astonishment, "I hadn't thought of that!"

"I don't believe you had," he answered briefly.

And again there was a silence—almost a frightening one.

"You know what people will say," he went on after a moment, "but I don't suppose you will care. You stood up to the gossip when your young man was killed—you can face it again with me."

"Are you . . . saying . . . that we could just . . . be together . . . without . . ." I stammered and couldn't go on.

"You shall do what you want to do," he answered. "I will accept any terms you suggest."

I felt like a business contract, but I replied:

"I would like to be with you . . . I would like it very . . . much but . . . if you could wait until . . . I am sure about . . . the rest . . ."

I paused thinking he might be angry and then it sort of burst out of me:

"It might . . . be horrid . . . unless we were . . . in love."

Sir Sydney just looked at me and said quietly:

"We will wait until you are."

I thought for a moment before I replied:

"But . . . supposing I don't ever . . . love you?"

"Then we will part with no hard feelings."

"Do you . . . mean that . . . really and . . . truly?" I asked rather breathlessly.

"I always mean what I say," he answered.

175

"And you do . . . want me . . . to stay . . . here?"

"I shouldn't ask you if I didn't," he said gruffly.

Then he walked across the room to his writing-desk by the window and unlocked the top right-hand drawer with a key which he carried on his watch chain.

Out of it he brought a little parcel.

"I got this for you yesterday," he said, tossing the parcel into my lap.

'Curiouser and curiouser,' I thought, like Alice in Wonderland.

I opened the parcel and found the most beautiful diamond watch bracelet I have ever seen. There was a tiny watch face set in absolutely huge diamonds.

"Oh, it is lovely!" I said with a gasp and put it on my wrist. "Did you really mean this for me? I can hardly believe it. I thought you didn't give people presents."

I got to my feet as I spoke and then very shyly I put up my face to kiss him.

"Thank you," I said, feeling rather like a small child approaching a severe schoolmaster.

I was so short with no heels and the top of my head barely reached to his shoulder so that he had to bend his head down to mine.

I had meant to kiss his cheek, but instead he kissed me on the mouth and funnily enough it was much nicer than I thought it would be.

He smelt of soap, eau de Cologne and cigars, rather a nice clean masculine smell.

Then I suddenly realised that under all his gruffness he was shy too, and that made me feel more at ease and not so young and unsophisticated.

I saw the funny side of it, of me and him and his strange proposal, I laughed.

"Do laugh, too," I said, "it is funny, really it is. This pompous house and you who everyone is frightened of, and me with no shoes and stockings, without a penny in the world, and this lovely bracelet . . . and oh, just everything!"

He didn't laugh, but he took my hand in his and held it very tightly for a moment.

"I like your courage, Linda," he said.

He would have said more, but at that moment the clock on the mantelpiece chimed the half hour.

"I must go," he said sharply, with his old brusque manner.

"That is a bargain, then?" he asked, as if I had sold him something over the counter.

I didn't have time to think or reason with myself, I just nodded my head, and before I could say any more he kissed me again—this time on the cheek—an awkward rather hurried kiss, and had gone from the room.

I was sitting pulling on my stockings, which were dry, when the butler came in.

"Sir Sydney has ordered the car for you in five minutes, my Lady," he said, "and would you mind calling at Barclay's bank before three o'clock? He has telephoned instructions."

That is just like Sir Sydney's efficiency, I thought.

But when I arrived at the bank and asked to see the manager I was completely stunned.

For he told me that Sydney was making arrangements to transfer a large sum of money to my account, but that at the moment I could draw up to five hundred pounds.

"Five hundred pounds!" I ejaculated, but the manager seemed to take it as a matter of course.

"How much would you like in cash at the moment?" he asked.

He seemed quite disappointed when I wouldn't have more than just enough to pay the rent and leave myself with a few pounds over.

The die is cast now, anyway, I thought to myself, and I drove back to the flat.

I gave the rent downstairs and at the same time I told them I should be leaving to-morrow. I couldn't go to Cressaway to-night.

I had to have one more night in the room where I have been so happy with Harry.

I can never expect to be as much in love again, there will never be a second Harry in my life. But in some funny way it is almost an adventure, this Sydney business.

I don't know him at all well and he is so utterly different from anyone I have ever known. I don't feel that there is the same disloyalty to Harry as if I went away with a young man whom I loved and who was in love with me.

At the same time I have a queer feeling that although I

haven't any money I can still give Sydney something which he can't buy.

I shall try to make him happier; nothing could be more ghastly than being alone in that great ugly house. And I am sure, if nothing else I can make his surroundings prettier and less lugubrious.

When I dined there to-night I couldn't help saying that I hoped he would allow me to change some of the rooms.

"Time enough for that," he answered, and then he added, "Oh, you can brighten things up a bit if you want to. I expect you will go on until you get your own way, so I might as well give you a free hand to start with!"

Sydney has a queer grudging way of being nice to me, as if he resented wanting to.

I have a feeling that if we ever had a row he would be angry not because of what I had done, but because I was capable of having any power over him. He has been top dog for so long that I am quite certain he is almost resentful of the fact that he wants me with him.

I can see that I am not going to have exactly an easy time. In a way it makes it so much better. I should like it to be difficult. I shall feel that I am earning my keep and that I am not entirely a debtor.

All women fundamentally like to give. The moment they are in love they would rather not take anything from their man—while those who are gold-diggers are driven to it by disliking the men who run after them.

After I had been to the bank I rushed round to Cantaloupe's and told Cleone everything that had happened.

She was so surprised that she couldn't believe it at first.

"It's a joke, Linda," she said, "you are pulling my leg!"

And when I assured her that I wasn't, she said:

"Well, you are just the luckiest person in the world—you certainly fall on your feet. Why he is the richest man in England, or nearly."

"Do you know, Cleone," I said, "I do like him—I do, really. I believe that under all his eccentricities he is one of the few real people I have ever met since I came to London."

Of course, Cleone didn't believe me, I could see that, although she was too sweet to say so.

She thinks that Sydney is terrifying and though she admires me for being clever enough to get him, she doesn't believe there is any more to it than that I have been after a rich man and managed to hook him.

I didn't tell her of our bargain and that we weren't going to be lovers. I just knew she wouldn't believe it!

After all, as I said to myself when I was dressing to-night, if Sydney is awful I can go away and leave him and there it is.

Cleone helped me choose a new dress at Cantaloupe's and Madame Jean let me have it to wear right away. Thank goodness they fit me.

It was such a relief to throw my old coat and dress into a corner and think I should never have to struggle with their threadbare and shabby appearance again.

Then I went downstairs to the accountant's office and wrote out a cheque for all I owed. And while I was there doing it, Mr. Cantaloupe himself came in.

"Hello, Linda," he said, "how are you?"

When he saw what I was doing he became even more affable.

"That is a big cheque to be writing all at once," he said socially.

I knew that he was just dying with curiosity to know who was backing it, but just didn't dare to question me.

"I am afraid I have owed it for some time," I said demurely.

I absolutely rushed round for the rest of the afternoon, and it was lovely to have a car to take me everywhere. I had my hair done, and I got some new evening shoes to match my dress.

By the time I had finished I had only just time to have a bath, dress and be at Cressaway House on the stroke of eight o'clock. Sydney, like most business men, is very punctual and he likes dinner early.

So I didn't have time to write to Mummy as I had intended to; instead I wrote her a cheque for twenty pounds, stuffed it into an envelope and sent it off.

I know how delighted she will be and if I can manage it to-morrow, I will write and tell her exactly what has happened.

I am sure she won't believe it is a platonic arrangement and will think I am living 'in sin'. But perhaps one day I'll get married again and then she will be happy.

I enjoyed my dinner with Sydney to-night and we made

all sorts of plans for to-morrow. We are going over to Paris for a long week-end first. I think it is very sweet of him to think of that.

There is something rather gloomy about the thought of my moving, boxes and all, into Cressaway House. As I have never been to Paris I shall be thrilled, and it really will seem like a sort of pretend honeymoon.

Lying here in the dark I feel a bit shivery down my spine when I think of it. To-night I am going to say good-bye in my thoughts once and for all to my memories of Harry. They are so precious and nothing and nobody in the world can take them away from me.

Harry belongs to me for all time, and the Linda he knew is his too, for ever.

But I am making a resolution here and now that I will try to repay Sydney for all his kindness and to make his life a little lovelier because he has met me.

And oh! I do like my diamond bracelet and I wonder what else he will give me?

REFLECTION FORTY

Paris is thrilling! Of course, travelling with Sydney is rather like being part of an Arabian Night's entertainment.

I had no idea that rich people could do things so comfortably, and it really makes me laugh to think of the days when I used to hide under the seat in the third-class carriages.

To begin with we travel with a complete retinue of servants.

There is Sydney's secretary—not Norman, but another one who manages most of his foreign affairs—there is Sydney's valet and my maid. The butler at Cressaway House found one for me.

A car and a chauffeur have also come over, and we were met and escorted by station-masters, railway detectives and superintendents on every possible occasion.

It really was rather exciting, and when we arrived at the Ritz and saw the suite we were staying in, I felt quite awed.

There were masses of flowers everywhere, ordered by Sydney's secretary, but he himself had thought of them, which I liked.

When we had changed and were ready for dinner, I

found he had a present for me. It was a huge cape of Russian sables. He must have written to the shop in Paris and had it sent round before we arrived.

I was most awfully pleased, not only because they were so marvellous, but also because they were a surprise present—the sort I like best of all.

I somehow imagined that Sydney might be the type of man who would say:

"Here is some money, buy yourself anything you want," which is not a bit the same as having special presents.

All the same, it seemed an awful lot of money to spend on me, as things were. So I said a little awkwardly:

"Do you think you ought to . . . give me so much when . . . we're only . . . only on approval, so to speak?"

"There are two ways of looking at it," Sydney replied almost as if I was in a board meeting. "First I want to give you presents, secondly as everyone will think you belong to me, they will think it extraordinary if I didn't."

I laughed.

"Either way it's heads I win—tails, you lose!"

"Do I?" he asked in a funny way, to which I could find no answer.

We had a marvellous dinner and then we went out for a little while to a very gay restaurant which is quite unlike anything I had ever seen in my life before, and I enjoyed myself a lot.

Sydney introduced me to all sorts of people—Frenchman mostly—whom he knew in business and they were perfectly charming to me, and I was really quite sorry when Sydney wanted to go home.

He was really awfully sweet and I think that he is really rather nervous of me, only of course he would rather die than show it.

He kissed me good-night in the sitting-room. A possessive but not passionate kiss and then we both went to our own rooms, mine was so elegant and filled with pink carnations.

Sydney had a lot of business to do to-day, and so I went off by myself to buy some clothes at the addresses Cleone gave me before I left. I have got some wonderful things!

At a shop in the rue St. Honore I saw some awfully attractive links and I bought them for Sydney, although it seemed rather silly giving him a present with his own money.

I do wish I had just a little money of my own. I think every woman must feel that, whether she is married or not.

One ought to be able to give one's husband or lover presents without them having to earn the money first. Although I don't suppose they look at it that way.

Anyway Sydney was delighted and he said that it was the first present he had had for years.

He must have known some awfully queer women in his life. Either they were just out for what they could get, or else what Norman says it true, that he hasn't looked at a woman for a long time.

I didn't believe Norman when he told me that, because I felt that anyone in Sydney's position must have known hundreds of women as he is such a virile personality.

But he seems so pleased whenever one is the slightest bit considerate and nice to him that I have come to the conclusion that Norman was right and that the only women he must have known were 'just brief interludes', as Cleone calls them.

I spent a lot of money on clothes this morning, and when I got back to the Ritz I felt quite embarrassed.

Sydney has given me thousands of francs and has also told me I could put as much down on account as I wanted and he would pay when the things arrived at the hotel.

Everything I have got was absolutely necessary. I simply had to have some new underclothes as well as dresses, shoes and hats, and I had only one pair of black gloves to wear and two pairs of decent stockings!

Even so I felt a bit shy when I found him in the sitting-room.

"I have a confession to make," I said, hoping that I was looking pretty, so that he would not mind so much.

"Well, what is it?" he asked abruptly.

"I have got quite used to his way of talking now; I realise that it is just characteristic of him and that he doesn't mean to be abrupt—it comes from years of getting down to the point and not wasting time.

"I have spent a fortune!" I said.

He frowned for a moment, and then he put his arm round my shoulders and tipped my face up to his.

"I will make another one, Linda," he said, quite lightly for him, "and you can spend that too."

Then he gave me a present—something I have wanted for ages and have never had—a really big solitaire diamond ring.

It is simply magnificent and must have cost hundreds of thousands of francs. I was quite speechless—I couldn't even say "thank you," but I think Sydney understood that I was pleased.

I walked about flashing it in the mirrors, and I could hardly bear to take it off even to get into my bath.

I can see it now twinkling on my dressing-table through the open door.

I do think it is marvellous of Sydney, and how anyone could ever have said that he was close-fisted I don't know.

I like him more every day and I think that he is happier, as I promised myself he should be.

And after all if I do leave him, I will give back all his presents.

REFLECTION FORTY-ONE

I know now what people feel like when they come back from their honeymoon.

It really is like coming back into the world, and it must be quite agonising if one loves somebody terribly.

It has been bad enough for me. We have now been home from Paris for ten days and to-morrow we go to Five Oaks, Sydney's house in the north.

I really enjoyed Paris, and even though we overstayed our original plans by a whole week, I could have wept when the time came to return to England.

I was excited though at the thought of seeing Cleone and showing her all my new clothes and presents. I had got her all sorts of lovely things too, which I knew she wanted for her trousseau.

I suppose really that half the fun of having things given to one is to show them off.

It was inevitable that I should find Cressaway House even more depressing than before. It is so large and gloomy, and after having been travelling most of the day I felt quite miserable as we sat down to dinner in the "mausoleum."

Sydney was rather cross and disagreeable too, having found endless messages on his return, and altogether we had the worst evening we have ever had together.

The bedroom, too, where I was to sleep was done up in the most hideous Victorian paper with heavy purple hangings and massive mahogany furniture.

I suppose that got on my nerves, and when we went up to bed, we had our first row.

It was a tactless moment for me to approach the subject of decorations and I ought to have known better, but occasionally one forgets to be diplomatic and is just natural. He came with me into my bedroom to say good-night.

"I think this is one of the most hideous rooms I have ever seen in my life," I said.

"What is wrong with it?" Sydney asked.

"The same thing that is wrong with the rest of the house," I replied.

"I am sorry it is not good enough for you," Sydney said sharply.

The next moment he turned and walked out of the room slamming the door.

I was furiously angry at that. If there is one thing that is irritating, it is someone going out of the room when one is in the middle of speaking to them.

I got into bed in a bad temper and lay there thinking horrid things about Sydney and about the bone of contention—his house.

The silly thing about thinking unkindnesses is that it hurts oneself so much, one gets all worked up and agitated.

And after a moment I found myself having long and bitter conversations in my mind—thinking I will say this and that to him and then he will say this to me, and then I will answer back . . . on and on and on, quite pointless and only making myself miserable for no reason.

I sat up in bed and listened. There was complete silence everywhere. The fire-light flickered on the huge mahogany chest of drawers and great wardrobe and cast dark shadows in the corners.

Suddenly I felt very lonely and miserable.

I would have given anything at that moment to have changed the grandeur of the house for my tiny room which I had left only a week or so ago.

I would have given a great deal to have run down the flight of stairs, visited Cleone and told her that I was unhappy.

As the fire sank lower and lower the shadows grew bigger and bigger until they were quite frightening. I expected a ghost to pop out of the cupboard at any moment.

The furniture cracked, and the blind, flapping in the wind from the open window, startled me.

I couldn't bear it a moment longer. I jumped out of bed and put on my dressing-gown and opened my door.

The passage was in darkness, but I crept down it to Sydney's room. Very cautiously I pooped in. There was complete silence inside.

His fire was even lower than mine and I could see nothing save the dim outline of his great carved four-poster. I couldn't even see if he was there.

Suddenly I felt terrified. It was like a nightmare, this big dark silent house! It was unfriendly, grim and ghostly!

"Sydney," I said in a whisper and then louder, "Sydney!" and then louder still, "Sydney, where are you!... I'm ... frightened"?

There was a movement in the shadows of the big bed, and then in terror I rushed across the room towards him.

"I'm sorry . . . I'm sorry," I cried. "I was horrid to you and I didn't mean to be . . . and you are so kind . . . to me."

He sat up in bed and put his arms round me and I hid my face against his shoulder.

"I'm an ungrateful beast," I whispered.

"You're nothing of the sort," he said quietly. "You just forgot I'm a crusty old bachelor who is not used to changes."

He held me rather tightly and said abruptly:

"You can alter the house any way you want."

"You ought to punish me by saying 'no'."

"But I have no wish to punish you. I want to make you happy."

"Oh, Sydney," I said with a little sob.

After a moment he asked:

"Are you happier than you were Linda?"

"You know I am much, much happier."

"Do you like being here?"

"I love it . . . except just now when I was frightened because you were angry with me."

I guessed he was smiling as he replied:

"Then I mustn't be angry, must I?"

We talked for a bit and then he kissed me good-night and I kissed him, really kissed him. It was so nice and comforting.

Then he took me back to my bedroom and tucked me up.

"Go to sleep Linda," he said. "I want you to be happy—try and remember that."

Then he walked away rather quickly.

I have spent the last few days choosing the colours and stuffs for carpets and curtains.

I am afraid it is all going to cost a terrible lot of money, but I will say one thing about Sydney, when he makes up his mind to anything the expense of it doesn't worry him.

It is Christmas next week and we are to spend it in the north. I am glad to say that Cleone and Norman are staying with us and two or three other friends of Sydney's, so we may, with any luck, have a really gay party.

I am not looking forward to my first sight of Five Oaks. Norman has already warned me that it is even worse than Cressaway House, and I expect that Sydney will be difficult about my redecorating that as well.

It is funny how one's outlook changes. I never worried what my room looked like before I came to London, and I certainly didn't worry when I was living with Bessie off the Tottenham Court Road.

It was Peter who first made me want to have lovely surroundings, and the funny thing is now I can't bear not to have them.

I suppose that is what people call culture—beginning by liking lovely things and then not being able to do without them, and getting better and better until one reaches a sort of perfection in taste.

I haven't been so silly as not to take expert advice on Cressaway House.

After all, if I was left alone, I expect I should make as many mistakes about house decoration as I did about clothes before I went to Cantaloupe's.

But the man who is doing all the work has agreed with me on lots of things although I told him to be quite certain to say if my ideas were wrong.

Sydney has been so busy that I have only seen him in the evenings and so I have had to go out by myself a good deal.

It is rather fun to have enough money to ask people to lunch with me for a change instead of having to be paid for. And it really does amuse me how awfully nice everyone is to me.

Of course, I quite expected to be cut, but as Cleone said to me rather bitterly:

"Money talks a good deal louder than brains or breeding, and you must remember that with Sydney's bank balance at your back you are a very social person!"

It is only the last two or three evenings that I have felt lonely and that has made me wonder how other people get on.

Silence is more frightening than anything I know, and silence between two people is even worse than when one is alone.

I expect really it is the sign of a weak character or something like that, and one should be so interested in oneself that one doesn't mind.

Perhaps if I am honest it is because I am just a little frightened of thinking.

REFLECTION FORTY-TWO

Norman was quite right. Five Oaks is terrible inside.

The house itself is really lovely, grey stone with gables, and if only Sydney would let me spend a little money on it I could make it absolutely charming.

He furnished it about twenty-five years ago and has never touched it since.

There are brass bedsteads in every room and frightful flowered wall-papers with dados and friezes. Most of the carpets are patterned and the curtains are draped and tasselled and keep the light out from the rooms.

The position is lovely and I really think I could be very happy up here.

I am going to learn to ride which excites me awfully, and I have already got a dog of my own—the most adorable wire-haired terrier.

The Christmas party went off very well and we really had grand fun.

I made Sydney let me have a Christmas tree so as to be able to give everyone their presents from it, and when I had cut off all the parcels there was one left, and it was for me—a lovely brooch.

I gave Sydney a new evening watch-chain, and I had

190

chosen a silver fox fur for Cleone with which she was absurdly pleased.

I had told Sydney what he was to give Norman and, although he grumbled, in the end he kept his promise and he gave him a cheque, which will cover the whole of the costs of Cleone's case and leave a bit over towards the furnishings of their new house.

Norman nearly had a stroke!

Their house is delightful. It is at the end of the park so that they won't feel overshadowed by Five Oaks. Cleone has not started to decorate it yet, it is empty, and I really envied her being able to start at the beginning instead of adjusting things that are there and camouflaging atrocities already perpetrated.

Sydney loves this house and I quite understand why.

He has always known it ever since he was a small boy working in the factory, and he used to trespass in the Park and grounds when he had a holiday.

One day he said to himself:

"When I am rich I will buy Five Oaks—it shall be mine—" and years later his resolution was to come true.

To-day, our first day alone, he asked me if I would like to go over the works, and, of course, I am longing to see them.

REFLECTION FORTY-THREE

We got to the works fairly early in the morning as Sydney had a meeting at eleven o'clock.

We drove through miles of narrow streets until we arrived there, skidding on the tram lines, once we only just missed killing some of the dirtiest children I have ever seen.

When we arrived at the factory we saw a large crowd of people standing outside. The car had to slow down. I thought at first it was some sort of demonstration. They were all men and they were all standing at the main entrance.

I have never seen such faces, terribly unhealthy and drawn. They did not seem to recognise Sydney; they looked at us in a dull, apathetic way, neither pleasantly, not hostile, just as though they didn't care much.

I had never seen people before with such a dead look about them.

"What are they waiting for?" I asked.

Mr. Simpson, Sydney's agent, was in the car with us. He is a dark, wiry little man with a hard face and rather shifty eyes. I have taken a great dislike to him, but Sydney says he is brilliant at his job.

No one answered my question for a moment. Simpson seemed to be waiting for Sydney, and then as he said nothing, he said:

"They are hoping for work, Lady Glaxly."

"All this crowd?" I asked in surprise.

"We took on ten new men this morning," Simpson answered.

We drove in, and as we did so, the men in front of the crowd made a movement as though they would come in after us, but they were waved away by the gate-keepers.

"Don't you want any more hands?" I said to Simpson.

"There is often a chance of one of the new lot being unable to stand the strain of a day's work, and that is why these other fellows are waiting," he said.

"Is your work so very hard then?" I questioned.

"It is if you have been out of work for some time," Simpson answered.

Then I understood why the men outside looked so strange.

Of course I had heard all about unemployment, but Sydney's factory had been doing so well that I did not imagine there was much poverty and distress in his particular area.

We walked all round the works, and I must say I think the machines were marvellous. I found the noise rather trying and I can't think how the girls and men can work there day after day.

But it was thrilling to see the great wheels turning and to see the raw material coming out as a finished article.

Simpson took me round while Sydney was at his meeting. It took hours, for we seemed to walk miles and miles.

The whole place was humming and buzzing with the noise of the machinery, everywhere people were hurrying about, and packers were working like lightning.

"We are employing nearly a thousand more work-people than this time last year," Simpson told me.

I found myself hoping that they would soon be able to employ all the men outside the gates. I don't know why, they seemed to haunt me.

When we came out they were gone, but we saw a lot of them hanging about the street corners, obviously with nothing to do, their hands in their pockets, in the most disconsolate, almost abject attitudes.

We drove back a different way from the one we had come by, because Simpson wanted Sydney to see a certain row of houses that had been condemned by the Inspector.

When I saw them I wasn't surprised—they were the most terrible places I have ever seen—absolutely filthy, and I can quite believe that they are verminous and insanitary.

"I wonder they haven't been condemned a long time ago," I said as the car pulled up. "And what about the ones on the other side of the street?"

I pointed them out as I spoke. They didn't seem to me as if they were any better.

Several poor looking women with shawls on their heads looked across at the car; they all seemed to have three or four children hanging on to their skirts, and generally a baby in arms as well.

"These houses are terrible," I said. "Why doesn't somebody do something for these people? Who owns this land?"

Neither of the men answered me, and then Sydney said grimly:

"Well, tell Lady Glaxly, Simpson, who owns the land."

"Sir Sydney does," Simpson said hurriedly and in a furtive manner, as if even he was ashamed to say it.

I didn't say anything, I just looked at Sydney. And then he gave an order to the chauffeur and we drove on.

All the way home I was silent. I was thinking over what I had seen, the terrible squalor, the dirt and misery, and it seemed to me awful that Sydney should allow it to go on.

After all, a little paint and a few repairs wouldn't cost him an enormous amount, and I know that the reports of his fortune are not exaggerated.

When we sat down to luncheon at Five Oaks, we were joined by two other men who had just arrived from America with plans of new machinery.

They were a blustering, rather voluble type of men, but I could see that underneath their self-assurance they were extremely anxious to ingratiate themselves with Sydney.

"We have sure got the goods for you this time!" the youngest man said. "This is the finest machine that has ever come out of the States, and that is saying something. It does everything short of washing the baby and putting it to bed—and we shall find one that will do that soon!"

Sydney grunted and helped himself to more *fois gras*.

He is never very talkative at the best of times, and he told me that he has often done more and better business by holding his tongue than by voicing his opinions.

"It's a big price, certainly," the second man said, "but look what it saves you in wages! Why, the whole machine can be under the care of one boy—all he has got to do is to pull a lever and it starts again with raw material and turns it out O.K. for the packers. Why, you save the wages of six men with this. Yes, sir! And if there is anything quicker on the market, I should like to meet it."

"Surely that means more unemployment?" I asked.

Everyone turned and looked at me in surprise, for it was the first time I had spoken since the meal started.

"Well, you won't get your employer to grumble at that, with Trade Unions forcing the wages up," the American said.

He seemed a little uneasy and kept looking at Sydney as if he was afraid that my remark might put him off the purchase.

Sydney hates talking business with me, he says he wants a little relaxation at the end of the day. But that night, I did ask:

"Did you buy that new machine to-day?"

"I haven't decided," he answered, in rather a reserved tone, which I know means he doesn't want to go on discussing the matter.

I can't help thinking that there must be some way to help those poor people. It is the memory of the men's faces that keeps coming before my eyes—that dead look as if they hadn't any hope left.

It is all very well to be pleased that Sydney's factory has done so much better, but I found out from Simpson that several others had gone bust last year and that there were literally thousands of men struggling to get work.

But Simpson is a hard, unsympathetic sort of person, and I bet he is the first to grind people down when they don't pay their rents. Anyway, he wouldn't tell me much about the place or if Sydney was doing anything for them, so I had to tackle Norman this morning.

"Sydney is tough, you know, Linda," Norman said when I asked him, "his reputation is pretty well earned, between ourselves. Not that I am saying anything against him," he added hastily, frightened that I might repeat what he had said.

"Now look here, Norman," I said, "anything you say to me is safe, I swear it. You don't suppose I would do anything to injure you in Sydney's eyes, do you? I just want to know, that's all.

"If you take my advice you will not bother any more about it, the whole thing is so vast—you don't suppose the Government are not doing their best—but you are too pretty to worry your head about it.

"I know the whole thing seems pretty awful the first time you come in contact with it—I felt like that myself, five years ago, and there was a prosperity boom on then.

"But you will learn not to notice . . . anything we could do would only be a drop in the ocean."

"You have never been really poor, have you, Norman?" I said. "I have. I have been hungry myself—not starving, but just uncomfortably empty. I have been without work, too.

"Only for a short time, but I know what it is like dragging round, hoping fiercely that at each new place one will be lucky and being disappointed time after time."

I ought to do something . . . I know I ought . . . but I don't know what.

REFLECTION FORTY-FOUR

We came back to London yesterday and I am absolutely delighted with the house.

My bedroom is quite lovely; in pale green with flame hangings and a huge gold and flame bed.

And the dining-room which I always loathed is one of the nicest rooms in the house, pine panelled and hung with cherry velvet curtains to match the chairs.

Sydney has agreed that I shall give a party next week, and I shall be able to use the drawing-room which has been shut up for years and years, and which I have now had completely altered.

Cleone was absolutely hysterical about the whole place when she dined here last night.

"Really, Linda," she kept saying, "I had no idea you were so clever! When I think of you coming to Cantaloupe's last year with crimped hair, the most terrible clothes and all the wrong make up, I can hardly believe this is you and your handiwork."

"I must do Five Oaks as well," I said to her.

When I mentioned the north I saw her face change, and a moment later, as soon as she began to speak, I knew that

Norman had been telling her what I had said about the factory.

"Linda," she said. "I don't want to interfere, or even offer advice that is not wanted, but you know, dear, how you have always paid me the compliment of asking me to tell you the truth, which I have always tried to do.

"And if you don't think me impertinent, I do feel you are making a terrible mistake if you try to interfere in Sydney's business.

"He is a funny man, Linda, and you will forgive me saying so, but he is known as the hardest landlord and the most severe employer in the country. You knew that before you went to live with him and you are not going to alter his business methods whatever you may do to his houses."

"Why not?" I asked.

"Oh, Linda, do be sensible!" Cleone said. "You have got a wonderful position now—you are safe—why jeopardise your own future?"

"In other words, you think that if I interfere with Sydney he will kick me out?" I said.

"Norman is afraid so," she answered. "Of course he knows that Sydney adores you and has been most awfully generous, but he won't stand interference from anyone. He had a secretary once—this was years ago now—and everyone thought she was indispensable to him.

"Oh, no, she wasn't pretty or anything like that," she added quickly, "but she was a sort of housekeeper-confidant to him and saw to all his business. One day they came to blows over some welfare work in the factory area and to everyone's horror he dismissed her with a month's salary—after years of service.

"Do think about it, Linda, and don't do anything stupid. After all we have all got to think of ourselves, haven't we?"

I have been thinking over what Cleone said, and I must own that her story as well as her fears have shaken me a bit.

I wonder if Sydney is really fond of me and if I mean anything to him, or if I am just a passing interest whom he will dismiss at the first disagreement.

I have a feeling that I mean more than that. Not only because he is terribly generous to me, but also because he is quite considerate at times in an almost tender way—that seems an absurd word to use where Sydney is concerned—

but he is sweet to me.

I don't mind his bad temper. He still rants at the servants and at me sometimes, but I suppose I got innoculated against that sort of thing by Alfred.

It used to terrify me as a child the way he went on at Mummy. But now when Sydney shouts and bangs the table and loses his temper, it just makes me feel rather calm and unmoved.

I think that not only surprises him, it makes him almost respect me. I am quite certain that if I cried or lost my temper too, it would be much worse.

As it is, after the first outburst he glares at me in silent fury and then gradually subsides and becomes quite tractable and reasonable.

I am free and I am a widow!

Pimples was killed in an earthquake in Japan! I suppose I should be upset and sorry but I can't pretend what I don't feel.

I had really forgotten him and I find it difficult now to even remember what he looked like.

REFLECTION FORTY-FIVE

Three days ago I dropped Harry's diamond ring into the Serpentine. I watched it vanish into the water.

I could hardly bear to part with it, yet I felt it was wrong to keep it, because every time I saw it I remembered Harry.

I am getting more sensible and I realise that it is no good hankering after the impossible. Harry is dead as far as my life is concerned.

I have tried to lock his memory right away in the very depths of my heart. It is very precious and very beautiful and I keep it there for a rainy day or for when I am old and nobody loves me any more.

But for the daily round and common task, so to speak, it does seem to me that I am not doing myself or anyone else, any good by brooding.

As I have thought so often no one else will ever be quite the same to me.

I am happy with Sydney, and I am enjoying life enormously. My ring was the last link.

The other day I found myself complaining about the caviare, and suddenly in the middle of my grumble I laughed.

"What's the joke?" Sydney enquired.

"Me," I said, "or is it I, I can never remember. It makes me laugh to hear myself complaining about a brand of caviare—a year ago I didn't know such stuff existed!"

"Nonsense," he said, "you must have known that there was such a thing!"

"They didn't teach us to have luxurious tastes at the Convent," I answered. "We were always thanking God for small mercies—and very small some of them were, I can assure you!"

Of course I do think that being well off or rich is only a matter of comparison. I thought myself down and out when I had three pounds, I expect that would seem quite a lot of money to a man working in Sydney's factory.

I had forgotten all about those people until this moment, and now I can see their faces again. I wonder if I asked Sydney about them if he would talk, or if, as Cleone thinks, I might infuriate him.

He is a funny person about some things. At times I think I know him so well and at others he seems a complete stranger.

He has never mentioned his wife to me, and yet he has often said how much he would have liked to have children —a son to inherit his business and his money.

I have half thought at times that he was hinting at my having one. I really wouldn't mind—I would like to have a baby.

Would it matter if it didn't have a name? I am illegitimate and it doesn't seem to have affected my career much one way or the other.

It is money which counts these days and if it was Sydney's son or daughter, the child would certainly not suffer for lack of worldly goods.

I really wouldn't mind having one, but I don't think I could suggest it to him. It would be awful if he said "no".

I should always think that he didn't consider me good enough or something like that, and that might make us hate each other.

I wonder if that is what he meant? I wonder?

REFLECTION FORTY-SIX

Such a lot of things have happened that I have hardly had a moment to myself to think about anything.

Sydney disappeared after dinner and I couldn't imagine what he was doing.

'I wonder where he is?' I thought to myself, as I went down the passage towards Norman's office.

I was just going to open the door when Norman himself came out.

"I will telephone from upstairs, sir," I heard him say.

"Hello, Linda," he added as he closed the door behind him. "You can't go in there."

"Why not?" I asked. "What is happening?"

"Simpson has just arrived with the manager and secretary from the factory, and they are in conference," he said.

"At this hour?" I exclaimed. "Good heavens, surely they could have waited to see Sydney in the morning—it's nearly twelve o'clock."

"Strike time is any time," said Norman sourly.

"Strike time?" I echoed.

"Yes, yes," Norman said impatiently. "It is always the same, I have been in two or three of them before, and

Sydney is up all night and everyone else who works for him!"

"But is there a strike?" I questioned.

"Heavens, hasn't he told you ... don't you read the papers?"

By this time we had reached the Sitting-Room upstairs, and Norman was dialling TRUNKS.

"I haven't read the papers for days," I said, "what with all the arrangements for this party, I don't seem to have had a moment."

"Well, don't say I told you about it," Norman said, "Sir Sydney may not want you to know. Though if he had meant it to be kept a secret I expect he would have said so."

I found a short paragraph in the *Evening News* which said:

> *"NEWS OF THE STRIKE AT THE WREX FACTORY. The deadlock between the employers and employees still continues. This makes the fifth day of the Strike and unless an agreement is speedily reached, there will undoubtedly be distress in the district. Owing to the strikes in the Spring and last year, the Union relief funds are being rapidly exhausted. A deputation of strike leaders are reported to be willing to open negotiations."*

"What is Sydney doing about it?" I asked Norman.

"Sitting back and biding his time," he answered. "He can afford to."

At that moment the call came through.

"This is private, Linda," Norman said. "Do you mind?"

I left the room and it was another hour before Sydney returned.

"Everything all right?" I asked.

"Perfectly," he replied shortly; I would have seized the opportunity of discussing the strike with him, but he went on.

"I am not going to talk, little one, I have got a hard day's work in front of me to-morrow and I must get some sleep. Good night, bless you."

He kissed me good night and was gone almost before I could answer him.

I was so tired that I fell asleep almost as soon as my

head touched the pillow, and the next thing I knew it was ten o'clock and my maid was pulling the curtains.

I opened my eyes and stretched, and then, beside my breakfast tray, I saw a note in Sydney's handwriting. I sat up and opened it quickly.

> *"I have had to go north on the early train. I shall be back as soon as possible. I will telephone you to-night. Don't worry about anything except looking after yourself.*
>
> > *Sydney."*

All day I wandered about wondering what was happening, wishing I had gone with Sydney.

Every time the telephone rang I hoped it was him to say that everything was settled and that he was coming home. At nine o'clock Sydney got through to me.

"What is happening?" I asked at once.

"Everything is quite all right," he answered.

"You mean it is settled?" I questioned.

"No, but it will be soon," he replied, "and on my terms."

There was silence for a moment, and then we talked about other things, and when he had said good night and had rung off, I sat for a long time staring into the fire.

I felt I ought to be up there with Sydney even if he would not let me interfere.

The poor wretched children with white faces and sores came into my mind. They would be the ones who would suffer. If the Union money completely petered out what would happen to them?

Quite suddenly I came to a decision. I rang the bell for my maid and when she came sent her for a Bradshaw.

I found there was a train leaving London at midnight— a sleeper which got in at seven o'clock in the morning. I told the maid to pack and get ready.

I don't know why, but something prevented me from ringing up Sydney.

'I will go as a surprise,' I thought, and I didn't even ring up Cleone, knowing that in loyalty to Norman she might betray my confidence and tell him I was on the way.

I couldn't sleep in the train, although I was very comfortable. I lay awake hour after hour, and it seemed to me that the wheels kept saying:

"What are you going to do? What are you going to do?"

Cleone's warning, and Norman's, kept coming to my mind and I found myself arguing with myself.

"You little fool, Linda," I said to myself, "why don't you leave well alone? People must look after themselves in this world. You have managed to, haven't you? If people have got courage they can get anywhere. You can't have courage on an empty tummy. I seem to remember thinking that before . . ."

I had lines under my eyes when we arrived and, anyway, I am not at my best when I get up at six-thirty in the morning. I pulled on my brown felt hat and wrapped my fur coat closely round me. There was a cold wind whistling round the station.

Of course there was no car to meet us. I put my baggage into a ramshackle taxi and then, at the last moment, I said to my maid:

"Go on up to Five Oaks and wait for me there. I am coming on later."

She looked at me in a scared way as if she thought I was up to no good. I called another taxi and I said to the man:

"Is there a Welfare worker in this town?"

He scratched his head and then he said:

"I don't know that there is."

"If you wanted to help the poor in this place, who would you go to?"

He spat.

"There are not many people who want to do that hereabouts," he replied.

"Do you mean to say no one is trying to help?" I asked.

"Well, the Vicar," he said slowly, "he does his best."

"Take me to him," I commanded and got into the taxi.

We bumped along over the narrow streets which seemed even more squalid and dingy than I remembered them. It was a damp drizzling morning and the town seemed bleak and miserable.

Already there were groups of men at the street corners and children splashing their way in broken boots along the wet and dirty pavements.

The Vicar's house stood back from the road beside a small grey stone Church, called St. Mary's. It seemed little better than the other houses in the town.

The linoleum in the hall was faded and broken and the wall-paper was peeling off in the sitting-room into which I was shown. The furniture was cheap and ugly, and festoons of coloured paper hid the unfilled fire-grate.

"If he is anything like his room," I thought, "he is not going to be much help to me."

Then the door opened and a man came in. He was young, dark and serious with a rather fine, almost handsome face, if he hadn't looked ill and slightly consumptive.

His clothes were threadbare, but the handshake he gave me was firm and sincere. Almost immediately I took a liking to him.

"You asked to see me?" he said, obviously surprised at my prosperous appearance.

His visitors must usually have been of a very different type.

"I have come to ask your advice," I said, "but before I start, would it be possible for me to have a cup of tea? I have only just arrived off the train."

"I am just in the middle of breakfast with my sister—if you wouldn't mind joining us we could talk afterwards," he said.

I not only wanted the tea, but I wanted to be sure of my ground before I started. I had come there on an impulse and felt rather frightened.

What was I doing? What did I desire to do?

The Vicar opened the door into a tiny back room.

A woman rose as we entered. She was rather like him in appearance, only healthier looking, and with a kindly bustling manner which was rather attractive.

"My sister," he said, "Miss Weston. And your name is . . .?"

"Glaxly," I answered. "Lady Glaxly."

I saw a flicker in his eyes which told me that he recognised the name and that he knew who I was. But they made me as welcome as they could.

His sister poured out tea, and apologised that they could only offer me bread and butter and marmalade.

I was quite hungry and glad to accept whatever they offered me, but after the first taste I knew that butter was a very pretentious name for the cheap margarine with which I spread my bread—I had had it too often not to recognise the taste.

The tea was good and hot and in a few moments I felt ready to start.

"I want you to tell me the truth—is the distress from the strike very bad at the moment?" I asked.

"I am afraid it is," said the Vicar. "You have asked me to tell you the truth and I won't mince words. The men are in a pretty desperate state, and their families are worse. A large number of them have been in and out of work for some time and all their reserves have gone."

"And the relief fund?" I asked.

"It was stopped yesterday," he replied. "My sister was working amongst the women and children all yesterday and will be doing it again to-day.

"We have got a soup kitchen for them, you know, but unfortunately our funds are very low and we don't know unless help comes, how long we can carry on."

"It is not only the children," Miss Weston interrupted, "it's the women too. Some of them are really ill, they have been denying themselves for weeks, anyway. And many are pregnant. But we daren't even start to help them for fear of depriving the children."

"If I get some money, can you get an organisation going at once to help the women and children?" I asked.

We couldn't do anything for the men, I realised that, but there was no reason why the children should suffer.

The Vicar's eyes lit up.

"Do you really mean that, Lady Glaxly?" he said. "If we could only give them soup it would be better than nothing, although milk is what the younger children need most."

"They shall have soup and milk," I said, "I swear it, whatever happens. I only want to know if you will do the organising."

"Oh, gladly, gladly!" Miss Weston said. "I can't tell you what this means, Lady Glaxly. I can't explain unless you have seen the women and children waiting and praying for this terrible strike to end."

And then, somehow, I found that they had both got hold of my hands and were shaking them, and there were tears in Miss Weston's eyes and a suspicious moisture about her brother's.

Outside my taxi was waiting, and when I told him to drive to Five Oaks he spat expressively on the ground, but he said nothing.

We drove creakingly down the road and all the time I was thinking of what I had done, and at the thought of Sydney my courage failed and began to ooze away from me. I was frightened of him, and I knew it.

"Well, he can't hurt you," I thought to myself; "if the worst comes to the worst you will be back again where you started, and something will turn up—it always does."

When I got to the house I went straight to my bedroom and washed my hands and tidied my face, and then I felt calmer and braver.

When I had done that I walked downstairs to Sydney's study, where I knew I should find him. As I expected he was there working at his desk, with his breakfast on a tray beside him, which was his habit when in the north.

He was alone when I opened the door, and I stood for a few moments waiting for him to look up.

"Linda!" he said in astonishment, springing to his feet. "What a surprise—why didn't you tell me you were coming? Why have you come?"

He walked towards me.

"Don't kiss me, Sydney," I said. "I had better tell you why I have come first."

"Well?" he shot at me sharply.

"I have come," I said slowly, praying that my courage would not give out, "I have come, to help the women and children down there in that filthy, beastly town of yours!"

For a moment Sydney didn't speak, and then he turned and walked back to his desk. He sat down and I advanced until I was standing in front of him.

"So you have come to interfere," he said slowly, thrusting out his lower lip.

"I am not interfering with the men," I said. "I don't understand business and I don't want to. But I do know what it means to the women and children and I am not going to stand by while you win the battle because they are starving."

Sydney put a cigar into his mouth and lit a match. He didn't speak and I felt myself shaking as I stood watching him.

"So *you* are going to help, are you?" he said with emphasis. "And may I ask who is going to pay?"

I had expected this and I had my answer ready. I took my huge solitaire diamond off my finger, unclasped my diamond watch from my wrist and the brooch which Sydney had given me for Christmas from the front of my dress, and put them on the table in front of him.

"You can give me the cash for those," I said, "and when that money is exhausted there are my sables. This won't cost you a penny. And if you won't give me the money I will take them to someone else who will. I have come to you first because . . ."

Then I faltered. I couldn't talk any more for tears. I stood silent, my eyes wide open to prevent the tears from falling out, gripping my hands together in an effort for control.

"And if I refuse to give you the money," Sydney said, "What then?"

"I shall still . . . get it on my . . . jewellery," I answered defiantly. "You can turn me . . . out of course you can but it still won't stop me . . . I shall still help those . . . people down there, even if it reduces me to the same state of . . . starvation as . . . they are."

I gave a little sob.

"You have ground these people . . . down but you can't do that to . . . me. I will have my own way over this and you can't . . . stop me."

Slowly and deliberately Sydney took out his note case and handed me notes to the value of fifty pounds.

"I will have the rest paid into the bank in the town in your name," he said.

Then, as I took the notes, he pushed back his chair in a fury.

"Get out and be damned to you!" he shouted.

I rushed out of the room and when I got outside I leant against the wall shaking with tears and trembling all over.

"I have . . . done it . . . now," I thought to myself.

REFLECTION FORTY-SEVEN

I have never seen people so thrilled and so excited as the Westons.

They could hardly believe their ears when I told them there was almost unlimited money, and they could do everything possible for the children and mothers.

They promised not to do anything for the men, for I meant to keep my word to Sydney.

Miss Weston had got together a large number of helpers, thin anxious little women who looked to me as though they needed food themselves, and within a few hours we had various depots in the town opened with food for the children.

I went to one myself and helped ladle out great bowls of soup containing pieces of meat and dumplings, so that it was rather like rich stock.

We gave them this with a piece of bread, and a glass of milk for those under five.

I have never seen children gobble their food at such a rate, or anything more pathetic than the mothers who queued up, most of them with a baby in their arms, and in many cases another obviously on the way.

Miss Weston lent me an overall, which I put on over my

fur coat, which made me look absolutely enormous.

It was not only for the sake of keeping myself clean, it was also because I didn't want to look too rich amongst that poor crowd who had hardly a respectable pair of boots or a warm coat between them.

But one didn't have time to think. It was ladle, ladle, ladle for hours . . . until the soup gave out. Even then there were rows of people who had to go away until replenishments arrived and we could start again.

Things are going to be easier to-morrow. It was only when I had finished that I realised how tired I was.

I had managed to snatch a cheese sandwich and have a cup of cocoa with Miss Weston and the others, but beyond that I had had nothing to eat since my cup of tea in the morning.

However, I couldn't give in, especially as they were all prepared to go on working until midnight if necessary.

As soon as the soup was ready and the milk had come, we opened again, ladling, ladling, ladling for what seemed an eternity.

They brought all sorts of queer things to hold their soup in; mugs, bowls, tins and old jam jars. One child brought a beer-bottle.

I was feeling in a haze, and my head was throbbing when suddenly Sydney's chauffeur appeared. He came up to me.

"Sir Sydney has sent the car for you, my Lady," he said.

My first impulse was to refuse and then I knew that it was quite impossible for me to go on much longer. Miss Weston saw what had happened and came across to me.

"I can manage now," she said, "there are not many left, and we shall have to close for the night. Good night, my dear, and God bless you for what you have done."

I staggered rather than walked to the car, and I suppose I must have fallen asleep from sheer exhaustion, for the next thing I knew was that we were back at Five Oaks and the Chauffeur was bending over me.

"You are home, my Lady," he said in a rather scared voice.

I got up, more dead than alive, and went up the white steps of the house. As I entered, the library door opened and Sydney came out.

I must have looked odd with an overall over my fur

coat and my hair all dishevelled.

I looked at him for a moment then suddenly the walls of the hall closed in round me and with a little groan I fell forward . . .

I found myself lying on my bed and my maid was giving me brandy to drink.

After a few moments I staggered up and in a complete daze let her undress me as if I were a little child. Then I crept into bed.

My whole body ached and ached and I was too tired to think of food. However, a little later she brought me some soup. I drank it. I told her to leave me alone.

"I want to sleep," I said.

"Are you quite certain you're all right, my Lady?" she asked. "You did give us a turn."

"I am all right," I answered, "I am going to sleep—leave the bell so that I can reach it."

I must have dozed for a little while. The sound of the door opening aroused me. I sensed that someone was standing looking at me, and with an effort I turned my head.

There was Sydney. I could see him in the firelight, but I could not see the expression on his face.

Was he angry wtih me? Did he mean to turn me out? Had he come to tell me to go?

All these thoughts rushed through my mind and somehow I felt too tired to cope with any more. I put out my hand feebly towards him.

"Are you . . . very angry with . . . me, Sydney?" I whispered.

He came across the room towards my bed and stood towering above me.

My heart gave a sudden leap of fright. I felt I couldn't bear a scene, I was so tired and so very, very weary.

"Am . . . I to . . . go?" I asked weakly.

I had to know, I had to have his answer.

He took my hand in his. Suddenly he knelt down beside me, and then Sydney the severe, Sydney the terrible, pressed his lips very tenderly against my cheek.

"How do you think I could do without you, my Linda?" he asked gruffly.

REFLECTION FORTY-EIGHT

Coming back from helping the Westons, I heard men shouting in the streets that the strike was over!

It had been a tiring day but I was not so exhausted as I had been yesterday. I haven't seen Sydney since he told me he couldn't do without me.

I was so tired I just fell asleep with my hand in his and when I woke up it was morning.

But in the car I thought about him and suddenly I knew that if he had sent me away I couldn't have borne it.

Quite unexpectedly he was my whole life, and he mattered more than anyone else.

It was as if slowly, so gently I hadn't realised it, he had crept not only into my very existence but into my heart.

Not like a flash of lightning, but like the dawn sweeping away the night, I knew he mattered desperately to me.

I wanted him to like . . . no love me . . . I wanted him to kiss me . . . I wanted to give him real happiness the sort he had always missed.

I know that I love him and have loved him for some time but in such a different way to the love I had for Harry that I hadn't recognised it.

I feel I've been very selfish in letting Sydney do so much for me when I have done nothing for him.

I have taken, and taken, and been so wrapped up in my memories of Harry, that I never thought that perhaps Sydney wants to have memories too!

I wonder if he is really fond of me—if perhaps he loves me?

He is such a difficult person to know and to understand and yet he can be so sweet and tender.

Perhaps he does love me in his way.

How shall I find out? What shall I say?

REFLECTION FORTY-NINE

I am so happy ... everything is wonderful ... wonderful!

I got home and I thought that Sydney would be back early as the strike was over, but he wasn't, in fact he was nearly late for dinner.

We dined alone and we talked very little while the servants were in the room.

I had taken a great deal of trouble to put on a dress I knew he liked and after dinner we went into the smallest and most cosy of the sitting-rooms.

There was a big log fire and I turned down some of the lights.

Sydney sat in a big arm chair. He had a glass of brandy by his side and a cigar in his fingers. He looked I thought very handsome and masculine.

I felt a sort of surge of warmth towards him but it was mixed with nervousness because I hadn't yet made up my mind what to say to him.

He was silent for what seemed a long time. Then he asked:

"What is worrying you?"

I was surprised he was so perceptive because I didn't

think he had taken all that notice of me.

"I am so very . . . very . . . glad the strike is over," I said after a moment.

"That is what you wanted, wasn't it?" he asked rather grimly.

"Do you . . . mean . . . I helped a . . . little?"

"You've cost me a lot of money," he answered.

"Oh . . . Sydney . . .!"

I ran towards him, threw myself against him and put my arms round his neck.

"Darling . . . I am so glad! You are wonderful! So wonderful . . . I love you!"

It came out spontaneously without my thinking what I was saying. Then I felt him stiffen before he asked very quietly:

"Do you mean that?"

I hid my face against his shoulder.

"I have been trying . . . to find . . . a way to tell you so," I whispered.

He held me very close. Then he said in a strange voice I had never heard before:

"Will you marry me, Linda?"

I was so astonished I raised my head and stared at him wide-eyed.

"B.but I . . . t. thought . . . you . . .h.had . . ." I stammered.

"My wife died three weeks ago."

"Why didn't you . . . tell me?"

"I was waiting until you loved me."

I put my face down again.

"I do . . . I really do Sydney . . . but you needn't . . . marry me . . . if you don't . . . want to . . ."

"I want you more than I've ever wanted anything in my whole life," he said. "Enough to let you interfere in my business."

"Enough to . . . stop . . . a strike?"

"Exactly."

I took a deep breath, then when I was least expecting it, when a strange exciting happiness was creeping up inside me, I started to cry.

"Darling, what is the matter? What have I said to upset you?"

I had never heard Sydney so concerned.

216

"It's because . . . you are so . . . kind, so . . . marvellous to me and I want to do something for you, to love you . . . to give you . . . myself and a . . . son."

Then I couldn't say any more. Sydney was kissing me so that I couldn't breathe and I couldn't think.

It was all very wonderful!

REFLECTION FIFTY

I'm lying in the dark and Sydney is holding me close against him with my head on his shoulder, and I'm so happy I can hardly think.

I didn't know that love could be so utterly and completely marvellous.

I suppose having waited so long and "kept myself to myself" as Mummy might say, I was secretly rather apprehensive in case it was disappointing like my first kiss.

But it's more wonderful than I can ever put into words.

We were married very quietly by the Vicar of St. Mary's because I said to Sydney:

"Let's have no one, no one at all at our wedding."

"Why not?" he asked.

"I want just to be alone with you . . . and God," I told him rather shyly. "If there are guests . . . even Cleone and Norman . . . you know they will be thinking how lucky I am to be marrying you because you are so rich."

I paused.

"On our wedding day I want to think of you not as a wealthy tycoon, but just as a man . . . my man!"

Sydney put his arms round me.

"A man who loves you very much, Linda."

The Vicar was simply delighted to perform the ceremony and promised not to breathe a word to anyone.

I was so frightened the Press would hear of it; but when we arrived very early in the morning there was no one in the Church but Miss Weston who was playing the organ very softly and the man who pumped up for her.

Sydney had sent lots of white lilies for the altar, the candles were lit and it looked lovely.

I held Sydney's hand as we walked up the aisle and he said his vows very seriously in his deep voice, which was rather gruff so I knew he was feeling as emotional as I was.

I prayed terribly hard that God would bless us and that I would make Sydney a good wife and give him lots of children.

Then we drove away and Sydney had a private plane waiting to fly us to London.

We didn't want to stay in our own house and have congratulations from the servants, so we went to Claridges Hotel. They are used to Royalty, and all sorts of important Heads of State so they are very discreet.

Tomorrow Sydney is taking me to the South of France on a real honeymoon, which is terribly exciting.

We had dinner in our sitting-room—caviare, champagne and all the dishes I like best.

But when it was time to go to bed I felt very shy and after I had undressed and was in bed, I also felt frightened.

I had never asked Sydney about his love affairs but I thought perhaps he had made love with lots of sophisticated experienced women and might find me dull.

After all I know really nothing about it!

Sydney came in wearing his blue silk dressing-gown with his monogram on the pocket, which is very becoming to him. He looked years younger because he was so happy.

I watched him cross the room and he must have realised I was nervous because he sat down on the bed facing me, his eyes on my face.

"You are not frightened, my darling?" he asked.

"Not of . . . you," I answered in a very small voice, "but suppose . . . I disappoint . . . you?"

He smiled.

"You won't do that."

"I'm . . . afraid."

He took both my hands in his.

"Listen, my precious," he said. "I love you and I want you because you are the loveliest person I've ever seen."

I gave a little exclamation of happiness and he went on:

"But I love you in so many other ways. I love your courage, your honesty and your kind little heart. But I also love the way you look at me when you are being provocative and also when you are not certain if I am going to be angry."

He drew in his breath.

"I could go on all night, my Sweetheart, telling you in words how much I love you but there's a much easier way to make you sure of it."

I pulled him towards me.

"Make me . . . sure . . . " I whispered.

Then he got into bed, took me in his arms and kissed me slowly, passionately and very, very possessively.

And it was as if he gave me all the most wonderful, beautiful things in the world—the sun, the moon, the stars, the sea, the flowers. They were all there and I was a part of them.

I know now that love is divine and comes from God and while it's the most thrilling, rapturous sensation one could ever imagine, it also makes me want to be good.

I'm sure now that Sydney loves me as I love him. I didn't know a man could be so gentle and yet so wildly exciting.

We are no longer two people but one and I am madly, crazily, happy.

He's awake so I'm moving even closer to him to whisper:

"Please . . . please . . . Sydney darling . . . go on loving me for ever and ever!"